THE SPIDER:
THE MAN FROM HELL

MASTER OF MEN!

THE MAN FROM HELL

By Grant Stockbridge

POPULAR PUBLICATIONS • 2025

CHAPTER 1
DEATH IN THE HALL

THERE WAS just enough rain to diffuse the powerful rays of Wentworth's headlights into a million shafts of glistening luminance, and to make the dismal East Side street lamps look like witches' candles. Pedestrians moved swiftly, with heads down, anxious to get home for dinner before the real downpour came.

Richard Wentworth sat in the rear of the big Daimler limousine, in a shadow. Ram Singh, the swarthy, bearded Sikh who was much more than a chauffeur, drove slowly.

"Master," he said over his shoulder, speaking in purest Punjabi, "there is danger. I dreamed a dream last night. I dreamed that you walked in a dark place, and that the grinning face of Death floated at your side. Let me go along—"

"No," said Wentworth.

He glanced out of the window; they were passing the mouth of a dark alley between two tenement houses.

"Stop here," he ordered.

He waited a moment in the shadow of the interior, while a hurrying pedestrian passed.

"You know what to do, Ram Singh?" he asked.

The Sikh nodded. "I am to go back and keep constant guard over Miss Nita. She is to know nothing of what you do tonight."

"Guard her well, Ram Singh, for there will be terrible danger

They came every day—for
twelve more hours of sight!

THE MAN FROM HELL

from the moment that I step out of this car. Danger which may reach her."

"Have no fear, Master. Go with Allah."

The door of the limousine opened, and Wentworth stepped out to the sidewalk. Strangely, he was almost invisible as he glided across the sidewalk, disappearing into the alley. Anyone looking in that direction at the moment would have sworn that no one came out of the car. Ram Singh threw a last regretful glance at the alley—where there was nothing to be seen—and drove off.

In the darkness of that alley, one would have thought at first that there was not a soul present. Yet in one spot the shadows were darker than elsewhere. Almost in the shape of a man were those shadows, yet not quite human. For it was no longer the trim and debonair sportsman whom the social world knew as Richard Wentworth who was gliding down toward the rear of the alley, but a grim and spectral figure attired in swirling cape and low-pulled slouch-hat—a figure whose name had come to be a byword of hate in the far-flung lairs of the Underworld. There were cruel men of power—overlords of crime—who would have paid a fabulous reward to any informer who gave them the information that Richard Wentworth, millionaire, dilettante of the arts and letters, amateur criminologist and patron of numerous charities, was also… the Spider!

Tonight, the Spider was walking again.

Down at the end of the alley there was a paved backyard, with a fence separating it from the yards beyond. Ash barrels stood gaunt in the rain, and overhead a clothesline creaked on its pulley, loaded with washing. There was noise, too—the discordant, clashing tones of a dozen radios in as many flats, the voices of men and women, and the clatter of dishes.

But in the yard there was no movement. Only the vague outline of a shadow, which seemed to merge with the darkness.

A radio in a ground floor window was tuned extremely loud. The strident voice of the announcer floated out into the yard: *"… the toll of victims credited to that vicious criminal who calls himself Professor Secundus has now risen to one hundred and eighty. Within two days, one hundred and eighty residents of this city have been rendered blind in some strange and terrible way. The victims have nothing to say about their experiences, as if fearing some far more deadly punishment. Only one bit of information will they give— that they were blinded by one who calls himself Professor Secundus. Tonight, the whole city is asking one question: Who is Professor Secundus? The police, under Commissioner Kirkpatrick, are bending every energy to solving this ghastly mystery which threatens to throw the entire city under a reign of terror.…"*

THE SHADOW in the back yard had progressed imperceptibly as the announcer spoke. Now it was close to the cellar entrance at the rear of the tenement house. Here, a small boy was standing stiff and taut, just inside the cellar doorway, peering out into the night with frightened eyes.

The boy had curly hair and a thin, studious face—a face that was pinched and sallow. The lad's right leg was in a brace. His fingers were fumbling nervously with the buttons of his sweater, and his young face made a white blob in the night. He was expecting someone. But he was utterly unaware of the shadow that moved to his side.

The Spider edged closer, and spoke in a low, kindly voice.

"Don't be frightened, Tommy."

The boy jumped, and an involuntary cry escaped from his trembling lips.

A dark gloved hand rested on his shoulder, another hand covered his mouth, smothering the cry.

"Quiet, Tommy. No noise."

The hand came away from his mouth, and Tommy looked up at the grim figure standing at his side.

"Y-you—you're the Spider?"

"Yes. And you're Tommy Blair?"

"Y-yes, sir."

"Are you afraid of me?"

"N-no, sir. It—it's just that—that you scared me. I didn't know you were there. I thought for a minute it was—those others!" The boy shuddered. "It's *them* I'm afraid of, sir, not you. My brother Jack has told me about you—how good you are, and how you always help those in trouble, and never kill innocent people—in spite of what the police say about you."

The Spider's face was invisible under the down-turned hat brim. But his voice sounded as if he were smiling.

"Thanks, Tommy. You're a brave lad to come out here—knowing the danger. What about your brother, Jack? Where is he?"

"He—he's hiding in a flat in the house after the next. Sis rented it for him the day he escaped from prison. He dassen't come out. The cops are after him, and *those others*, too. Jack says

they'll get him, for sure. All he
wants is a chance to talk to you
before they kill him." Tommy's
voice choked on a sob. He
clutched the Spider's cape.
"Y-you won't let them kill him,
will you, sir?"

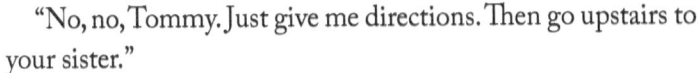

"I'll do my best, Tommy.
Now, tell me quickly where
that flat is—"

"I'll take you there, sir—"

"No, no, Tommy. Just give me directions. Then go upstairs to
your sister."

The boy pointed to the right. "It's the second house after this;
go through the yards. It's the rear flat on the third floor. Knock
three times, quick, then three times slow. Jack won't open to any
other signal."

"All right, Tommy." The Spider pressed the boy's shoulder.

Tommy hurried on eagerly. "Jack has told me and Sis a little
of what he found out from those men he escaped with. It—it's
about a terrible man who is called Professor Secundus—the
one who helped them escape. Jack only saw him once. He shiv-
ers every time he mentions the Professor's name. He says the
Professor is the most evil man in all the world, and if something
isn't done quickly, Secundus will control the whole city—"

The lad was growing more and more excited as he talked, and
the Spider suddenly stopped him.

"That's enough, Tommy! I think I saw something move, over

7

there in the next yard. Go upstairs quickly. Lock your door. Don't open it for anyone!"

He gave the boy a friendly push, and Tommy hobbled swiftly into the blackness of the basement. Out of the darkness the boy called back softly, "I—I hope I grow up to be like you, sir!"

Grimly, the Spider began to work his way across the yard. Virtually invisible himself, he knew almost at once that there were others in that next yard, equally silent and equally hard to perceive.

The house in which Jack Blair was hiding was being watched! MINUTES PASSED—MINUTES in which nothing in those yards seemed to move. But somehow, the Spider was suddenly at the rear of the building he sought.

From under the low brim of his hat, his two gleaming eyes searched the yard. There, behind a row of ash barrels, was a man, motionless, watching. And the swiftly falling raindrops glistened upon smooth metal—the barrel of a sub-machine gun. To that man's left, there was another crouching figure, sheltered behind an old discarded sofa. Both men were watching the back door into the cellar.

Up above was the room in which Jack Blair shivered in secret. Yet these men were not looking upward toward that window. They were watching the back entrance. Could it be that they knew the Spider was coming tonight?

Could it be that they were waiting for the Spider?

Wentworth edged back toward the adjoining house.

Silently, like a wisp of wind, he stole into the basement of the next building, and proceeded to the main hall. On the way, he pulled the switch controlling the electric lights in the hallway. He mounted flight after flight in the pitch blackness, reached the roof, and climbed out through the skylight. The people in that house would wonder about their hall lights, but they would never suspect that the darkness had been used to cover the ascent of the Spider.

The cloaked and shadowy figure crossed over to the next roof, climbed down through the skylight, and descended to the third floor. He moved swiftly here, because the lights were on, and one of the tenants might pass and cry out at sight of the frightening apparition.

The door of the third floor rear was closed. Behind that door, Jack Blair was hiding. The Spider stepped up to that rear door, standing sideways to it. Then he raised his knuckles and rapped—three times fast, then three times slow. Almost simultaneously with the sound of the last rap, the door of the *front* apartment, up at the other end of the hall, was yanked open.

A man appeared there. His face was partly hidden by the sub-machine gun which was raised to his shoulder. The muzzle swung toward the cloaked figure of the Spider, the man's fingers contracted on the trip.

CHAPTER 2
THE SPIDER'S SURRENDER

YET THE next sound in the hallway was not the staccato rattle of the machine gun.

Instead, there was a single deep-throated blast as flame

belched from a heavy automatic which had suddenly appeared in the gloved hand of the Spider.

The echoing reverberation of that thunderous detonation rolled through the upper floors of the building in a long, continuous chorus of thunder claps. And the man with the machine-gun went into a ludicrous back-flip as the heavy slug struck him dead-center in the forehead. His hands shot outward in a queer reflex motion, and the machine gun went flying out into the hall.

Behind him, in the front apartment, there were other men, and they pushed forward over their dead companion's body, with guns flaming in their hands.

But now, the ominous figure of the Spider was standing spraddle-legged facing them, with an automatic in each fist, and twin blazing lances flashed from their muzzles.

Just so had the Spider often stood, trading death with the shock troops of the Underworld. And through the years those twin blazing automatics of his had come to be portents of doom to those who faced them. His black-swathed body never moved. He did not deign to seek shelter from those who attacked. But his blistering slugs filled that doorway, laying down a barrage which carried death with the speed of light.

In a moment he ceased firing, and waited while the rumbling thunder of the gunfire marched up and down the halls of the house like a weird, macabre funeral dirge—a dirge for those in that front apartment who had thought to kill the Spider. For there were none left alive in there.

The whole building was bursting into panic. Women were screaming, and men were trying to quiet them, and the voices filtered out into the hall to mingle with the swift-retreating echoes of the gun blasts. None dared venture into the halls as yet.

The Spider moved swiftly now, and surely. He turned his back on the remains of those who had tried to trap him, and turned the knob of the rear apartment, where Jack Blair was in hiding. The door was locked. Blair had not come out, nor had he answered the Spider's signal.

With the frightened shouts of the tenants still in his ears, the Spider did not wait to be admitted. He knew well enough now, what he would find behind that locked door. He stepped back a single pace, and raised one of his automatics. There were still two cartridges in that clip, and he sent them both crashing into the lock. The flimsy door sagged open.

The Spider kicked it wide, and stepped in.

For a moment he stood just within the threshold, forgot the shouting and the cries throughout the building; forgot the keening of the quickly approaching police car siren—everything. He stood grim and stiff, his eyes burning with a sudden terrible intensity at the body of young Jack Blair, lying on the floor.

Blair was not dead. He was on his back; his hands and feet were bound, and there was a gag in his mouth. There was no blood, no sign of a wound. Yet something had been done to him. Something so terrible and despicable that the Spider shuddered.

He had been blinded.

There was no blood—only two empty and staring eyes. How

it had been done, it was impossible to tell. He was jerking spasmodically at intervals. This youngster who had been on the lam from the police would never escape again—for he would not be able to see where to go.

Swiftly the Spider knelt beside him and removed the gag.

Blair made feeble, incoherent sounds, interspersed with faint moans.

On the floor at his side was a black card upon which a message had been lettered in white ink. The Spider read it, but did not touch it:

"JUST SO WILL ALL THOSE BE SERVED WHO OPPOSE OR BETRAY PROFESSOR SECUNDUS!"

There was a strange and terrible note in the voice of the Spider as he put a hand on the shoulder of the blinded youth.

"I can't give you back your eyes, Jack Blair," he said bleakly. "But I swear to you that you shall not have suffered in vain. From this moment on, the Spider declares war on Professor Secundus—*war to the death!*"

THE THREATENING noises from without were drawing closer. Through the flimsy building walls could easily be heard the screeching of tires which gave warning that a police patrol car was pulling up at the curb. A clamor of voices arose. Men and women were directing the police.

"It's upstairs, officer. I think on the third floor… gangsters… murderers… men with machine-guns…."

Heavy feet began to pound on the stairs.

It was time for the Spider to go.

He could not afford to be trapped by the police any more than by those other, more deadly enemies who had planned his death here tonight. For the police, too, were the enemies of the Spider. For years he had lived in the dark and dangerous byways of independent crime-fighting—a lone-handed Nemesis of those criminals in high places whom the law failed to reach. But his very methods in dealing with these powerful adversaries were necessarily outside the law. And a long line of so-called crimes-had been laid at the door of the Spider. Should he ever be captured, his life would surely be forfeit in the electric chair.

Characteristically, though, he had forgotten the imminence of his own peril now, in the greater tragedy of young Jack Blair, lying delirious, helpless and blinded.

But one more second he must remain, even with the ominous tread of the police growing closer and closer. For he perceived that Jack Blair's lips were forming words. He bent close, listening, and heard only vague, disconnected words.

"Must tell the Spider... no one else can help... Samson's Grille tonight... Professor Secundus—that... devil...."

That was all Jack Blair said audibly. His voice became a mere whisper, altogether drowned out by the clattering din in the hall.

The police were at the second door now. Only a moment more and they would be here, would find the Spider stooping over a blinded man. And no matter what the note from Professor Secundus said, they would lay this crime also at the door of the Spider. It was the easiest way out for the police. Thus far, no one had been able to guess at who called himself Professor Secundus.

What could be simpler than to say that this was another vicious depredation of the Spider?

True, there were many in the city who would never believe it. There were many who at one time or another had occasion to find that the Spider was the champion of the underdog. There were many who swore by the Spider, remembering what he had done for them, and who would willingly lay down their lives for him. But not the police. Their duty was to capture this man.

The policemen from the patrol car were almost halfway up to the landing when the Spider rose from the now-still form of Jack Blair. There was no hint of panic in his movements. With a single swift gesture he flicked off the light. He shut the door, and slid a rickety dresser over against it. Then he crossed unerringly through the pitch-black room to the window and drew up the shade. His quick, strong, black-gloved fingers raised the window and he crawled over the sill to the fire escape.

Already the police were on the landing, and naturally, their first attention must be drawn to the dead bodies piled in the doorway of the front apartment. That gave the caped and cloaked figure on the fire escape an extra margin of time. He began a swift—descent. His cape swirled about him, and his hat-brim blotted out the whiteness of his features, so that he was nothing but a dark blob of shadow floating downward.

Yet there were those who saw him.

THE TWO men who had been lying in wait for him in the backyard were moving out from behind their shelter. They had seen the shadowy figure come out upon the fire escape. They were crossing the yard quickly at a run, which would bring them directly under the suspension ladder.

Looking down as he descended, the Spider saw them, saw the gleam of raindrops on the smooth metal barrel of the sub-machine gun in the hands of one of them. But he saw also that the machine-gun was not turned in his direction. And he understood that those men down there did not intend to kill him at once. That had no doubt been their intention when they were waiting for him to arrive. But now that he had eluded them and escaped the death-trap upstairs, now that he had had a chance to see Jack Blair, they wanted the Spider—*alive!* Because they wanted the information which Blair must have given him.

The Spider did not hesitate. He continued his descent. He had only one gun in which there were any remaining cartridges, but he did not even draw that. He came down conspicuously displaying his hands so that the men in the yard could see he was not carrying a gun.

Bleakly he smiled beneath the make-up of plastic material which distorted his features from the handsome face of Richard Wentworth into the ugly likeness of the Spider. This was such a chance as he had not expected to get—a chance to contact Professor Secundus. For if these men desired to take him prisoner, they would surely bring him to their master.

It was a long chance to take, because they might shoot him down when he reached the ground instead of taking him prisoner. But this man was used to making snap judgments in the stress of emergency, and then gambling his life on the soundness of those judgments. And now he was fairly certain that he was right, for if they had wanted to kill him out of hand they would have sprayed him with lead while he was an exposed target.

He swung down off the suspension ladder, let his feet touch the concrete of the yard, and let the ladder swing back up again.

The Spider glanced upward for one fleeting instant. The window of the room where Jack Blair lay was still dark. The police must still be occupied with the dead gunmen, still unaware that a blinded lad lay in the other flat—a lad whose young brother and sister were waiting with bitter anxiety only two houses away, sensing tragedy in the gunfire and the commotion they were hearing.

The Spider's lips were tight. He had made a promise to Jack Blair up there, and he meant to fulfill it—unless death should intervene.

He moved slowly now, as if unaware that men with deadly weapons were crouching just behind him. And he managed to assume surprise and panic when a hard gun barrel was jammed in his back, and a voice said, "All right, Spider, we got you cold. Don't move those hands!"

The Spider stiffened, with his hands at his sides. One of the two men came around in front of him, holding a revolver, while the other remained behind, keeping the sub-machine gun pressed against his back.

RICHARD WENTWORTH

"Fan him, Eric!" ordered the man in back. And then to the prisoner, "If you make a move, Spider, fifty slugs out of this drum will tear your backbone apart!"

Eric was a blond fellow of about twenty-eight, with soft, flabby features and weak, watery eyes. His hands were shaking a little as he searched the cloaked figure and took the two automatics from him.

"Gawd, Rolf!" he said to the man with the machine-gun. "It—it surely is the Spider. Imagine—we caught the Spider!"

Rolf chuckled. "Yeah. The Professor will like this a lot!"

UP ABOVE, in the third floor window, a light appeared. The police were in there now. In a moment....

Rolf prodded the Spider. "Let's go!"

The two gunmen got on either side of the cloaked figure, guided him toward the back fence. Behind the ash barrels there was a small opening where several boards had been ripped out. Eric stooped and crawled through first, then Rolf motioned for the Spider to follow.

"No tricks, now!" he warned. "You're too slippery to take chances with. The first thing you do that looks funny—and Eric or I will give it to you on the spot!"

"You needn't worry, my friend," the Spider said. "I shall not make any trouble."

"Huh!" sneered Rolf. "And they said you were tough!"

The Spider did not reply. He got down and crawled through effortlessly.

Eric was waiting on the other side, with his gun dangling loosely in his hand. His flabby face was terror-stricken, and there was a sort of film over his watery eyes. Almost before the Spider was on his feet, Eric seized him by the arm. Words tumbled from his lips in a frenzied whisper.

"Here—hit me and run! Get away! I'll say you took me by surprise!"

The Spider frowned. "You want me to escape? Why?"

"Because you're the only one who can save us all from Professor Secundus. God! Do you think I *want* to do all this? If you don't save us, we're lost. If Professor Secundus kills you, then there's no hope—"

"If you hate and fear Professor Secundus so much, why do you work for him? Why not quit?"

"Oh, God, no! You don't know what you're saying, Spider. I don't dare to quit. He has me, that devil—"

He could say no more, for a thunderous voice boomed from the third floor window: "Stop, you! Don't crawl through there, or I'll shoot!"

Eric froze, moving close up to the Spider, against the fence where they could not be seen from above. That cop up there was calling to Rolf, and had not seen them. A powerful flashlight clicked on, and the beam of light lanced down on the other side of the fence, toward where Rolf was kneeling.

The Spider heard Rolf spit out a curse, and whirl. Though he could not see what was happening, he could guess that the gunman was raising his sub-machine gun. At the same time, Rolf yelled, "Eric! Shoot!"

But Eric did not shoot. He remained frozen, pressing against the fence, alongside the Spider. And as if in echo to Rolf's call for help, the service revolver of the cop up on the third floor began to thunder, and shot after shot crashed into the body of Rolf.

That cop was taking no chances on Rolf's pulling the trip on the machine gun. He emptied the revolver into the gunman's body, and then shouted triumphantly, "I got him!"

He disappeared from the window, evidently bent on racing down to see what he had bagged.

On the far side of the fence, Eric was trembling, blinking his eyes as if he had difficulty in seeing.

"What—what'll we *do?*"

"Come on," said the Spider.

HE TOOK the trembling man by the arm, and dragged him along the fence to the end of the yard. Then he pushed him down into an alley leading out to the back street. Behind them there was a cacophony of sound as people screamed information to each other, and newly arriving police tried to keep order in the crowd which was milling out of the building.

Grimly, the Spider pushed Eric ahead of him. But when they were almost at the mouth of the alley, about to step out into the street, Eric hung back.

"No, no! We can't go out there—"

"Why not?"

"B-because the rest of our men are waiting out on that street—with the getaway car. If they see me, with you in that cape, they'll—"

The Spider looked at him keenly, studying him.

"Eric," he asked, "are you on the level with me?"

"Yes, Spider, I swear it by all that's holy."

"Why are you afraid of the Professor?"

Eric dropped his weak, watery eyes. "I—I'm afraid he'll blind me. If—if I don't obey orders, I'll never see again as long as I live!"

Wentworth was about to smile, but he suddenly thought of Jack Blair. He did not laugh. Instead he said, "Tell me, Eric. Do you know who the Professor is?"

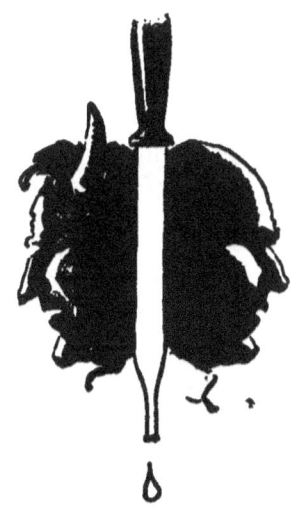

"God help me, no. I—I've seen him often—but he wears some sort of disguise over his face."

"Do you know where Professor Secundus' headquarters is?"

"No. Not that, either."

"Haven't you been there?"

"Yes. But every time I go, they blind me for a while, so I can't see anything. Then they fix it so I can see again, after we're inside."

The Spider stared at him quizzically. "They blind you?"

"You must believe me, Spider!" the weak-eyed Eric exclaimed earnestly. "I swear it's the truth."

"All right, Eric!" The Spider laughed suddenly, harshly. "Tonight, you're going to be a hero in the Professor's camp. Here, man, pull yourself together. Point that gun at me. You've caught me single-handed, understand?"

"But—but—"

"Do as I say!"

With shaking hand, Eric pointed the gun at the Spider, and got behind him. Then the two of them stepped out into the street.

A private ambulance was standing at the curb, with motor running. Two white-coated men who had been listening anxiously to the shooting from the back yard, sprang to attention when they saw the black-cloaked figure marching ahead of Eric. They sprang down, opened the rear of the ambulance.

"What happened?" one of them snapped.

"They got Rolf," Eric said. "But I brought the Spider. Boys, I got the Spider!"

The men grinned wickedly. They hustled the cloaked figure into the ambulance. One of the white-jacketed men got in the back with him, and dragged Eric in, too. The other jumped behind the wheel and started the ambulance. As they careened down the street with bell jangling, the white-coated men held a gun covering the Spider.

"Nice work," he said to Eric. "The Professor will like this. But the Spider won't. Mr. Spider, you're gonna wish they'd got you with the machine guns before the Professor gets through with you!"

The Spider looked appraisingly at this man, disregarding the quick, nervous breathing of Eric, who was also making a pretence of covering him.

"Tell me one thing," the Spider asked the white-coated pseudo-interne: "How was poor Jack Blair blinded?"

The fellow leered. "You'll find out about that, too!" he promised.

CHAPTER 3
BARGAIN IN BLINDNESS

T HE AMBULANCE was a new one, its chromium fittings glistening and shining. The springs and shock-absorbers functioned so well that no jolt was transmitted to the interior.

There were shutters on the two side windows, and on the glass in the rear door. Wentworth saw that these shutters were made of aluminum, and held in place by metal cross-bars which were set into an ingenious locking device. Thus, it was impossible to see where they were being taken. He looked around for some means of ventilation, and found a duct up close to the roof; it ran forward into the cab.

Wentworth was sitting on the cot along one wall, while the interne occupied a folding chair opposite. Eric sat on another folding chair which was attached to the back door. Thus, both men faced the Spider from different angles.

They looked at him curiously, inspecting the face of the Spider, which was known to them through having been caricatured in a thousand newspapers. He could see that they were nervous and excited at being in such close proximity to the famed and feared Nemesis of the Underworld, and they were taking this opportunity to get a good look.

Eric was sweating a little. Wentworth could see that he

23

had little confidence in the Spider's being able to accomplish anything as a prisoner in the stronghold of Professor Secundus. And Wentworth himself began to entertain his doubts. On the spur of the moment, it had seemed to him the only certain method of coming into contact with the vicious organizer of this terror campaign against the city. But now that he saw the elaborate precautions, the well-equipped ambulance, he began to think that perhaps he had underestimated Professor Secundus. If Secundus had deliberately planned to make the Spider a prisoner, then Secundus must surely have planned well and thoroughly.

Wentworth's thoughts raced back to little Tommy Blair, who must be waiting in dreadful uncertainty with his sister, wondering what had happened to their brother. Or, had they already found out? Did they know by this time, that Jack had been recaptured by the police, and that he would have to serve not only the rest of his sentence in blindness… but the rest of life?

The utter cruelty of Professor Secundus in thus throwing Jack Blair back, helpless and sightless into the hands of the law, was shocking. Wentworth looked forward with grim eagerness to the approaching meeting with Professor Secundus.

But he was not quite prepared for the manner in which the meeting had been arranged.

The ambulance slowed up, and turned into what must have been a driveway, then came to a stop.

The bogus interne was looking queerly at the Spider.

"Listen, mister, don't get any ideas behind that ugly mug of yours. Maybe you think we're takin' you to our main headquarters. Well, we ain't. The Professor ain't taking a chance of the Spider pulling a fast one and wrecking the whole set-up. See? So don't forget—this is only a branch!"

"I see!" said Wentworth. Behind the gruesome makeup on his face, his lips were thin and tight. He might have known that the Professor was far from a fool.

The interne was grinning in a nasty way. "And now, Spider, just take it easy. You ain't going to like what's going to happen to you now, but you can't help it. The Professor don't bother with blindfolds, or things like that. He goes right down to bed rock. See?"

Wentworth sat tautly on the edge of the cot, wondering what the interne meant, thinking fast, thinking hard. Eric, he saw, was sweating profusely, and trembling. He would be no help.

The interne was grinning. His face was taking on queer shapes, becoming elongated, then rounding out and widening, like a reflection seen in warped mirrors. His face was becoming blurred, spotty, transforming itself into a ghastly gargoyle that danced in the air, reminding him of the prophetic words of Ram Singh....

And suddenly, with a great wave of icy realization flooding his being, the Spider knew what was happening.

He was going blind!

THERE WAS a film in front of his eyes, and he could see nothing at all, not even the grinning face of the interne anymore. He heard the ambulance door open, heard heavy feet entering. Then he was seized roughly by powerful hands on either side, and hurried out of the ambulance.

THE SPIDER

The Spider was blind and helpless in the hands of his enemies.

No man is beaten until his courage is shattered, until the last glimmer of hope has ebbed from his soul. Before history began to be recorded,

it was known that Man was imbued with certain properties which distinguished him from all other animals. One of those properties was *faith*. Another has been the fierce will to fight against evil—to the last breath.

And as the race of mankind grew older, and began to write down in records the doings of man, those records became filled with examples of heroism—and faith.

Men still sing of Leonidas and those Spartans who fought at Thermopylae, of the Greeks who held the Persian fleet at Salamis, of Ulysses who met and conquered every obstacle on the face of the earth in order to reach home.

It was of another such example that Wentworth grimly thought as his two captors—whom he could not see—led him to the presence of Professor Secundus. He thought of Samson, who, eyeless among the enemy Philistines, brought the temple down upon their heads. Bleakly, Wentworth knew that, given the chance, he would do the same thing now. In every adventure he had ever undertaken, he had known full well that it might be his last. For no man is immortal, nor able to cheat death at every turn.

Some time, he knew, the end must come, and he was sure of only one thing—that when the inevitable moment arrived, he would trade his life as dearly as it was in his power to do. Blind or not, his ultimate goal in this war with Professor Secundus, did not leave his mind: to destroy this man of evil who brought misery, terror and blindness to the innocents of a great city.

He offered no resistance to those who led him. He wanted no fight with underlings. He must conserve every ounce of energy and cleverness for the struggle with the man who directed these pawns of crime. One ace-in-the-hole he had—Eric. He could not tell from the sound of the footsteps of those who accompanied him how many there were, or whether Eric was among them. But if Eric had come in with them from the ambulance, perhaps the youth would come through when the crucial moment arrived.

They took him along a corridor where the boards creaked, up three steps, then along another corridor. Presently they had to wait for a door to be opened.

Once within the building—whatever it was—no word was spoken. It was as if a grim army of the silent were marching with a bleak and unspeakable purpose. Even when they stepped into this last room, there was no sound of voice. When his captors released their hold upon his arms, and he reasoned that some signal must have been given. He heard them moving back, heard the door close softly. Had they left him here, alone?

His eyes were open wide, straining futilely against the terrible opaque film across them. He could see nothing; he could hear nothing. Yet he sensed now that there was another presence in the room. A full minute passed, and Wentworth stood poised and tense, all his faculties taut. And then he heard it—the faint sound of a chuckle... sinister, cruel.

A VOICE spoke. The voice was suave, educated, modulated— yet withal, inhuman. It was such a voice as might have belonged to the archangel, Satan, when he whispered his wily trickeries into the ear of the Deity, before he was cast out of heaven to become the Prince of Darkness.

"So!" spoke that arch-evil voice. "So this is the Spider. So this is the potent person who has struck terror into the hearts of criminals. See how helpless he stands before us. Deprived of his sight, he is no longer dangerous."

There was just the infinitesimal breath of a pause, and then Wentworth heard the voice continue.

"Observe, Lona my dear, that he is only human. You expressed worry that he might interfere with us. You see, there was no cause for worry."

Wentworth tensed as the tinkling sound of a woman's laughter, low-pitched and full-throated, echoed in the room.

"He is so funny," said the woman. "Standing there and straining to find where we are standing, and with his eyes so blank!"

Indeed, that was the very thing that Wentworth was trying to do. He was exerting every faculty to locate Professor Secundus and this woman called Lona. The presence of the woman disturbed him. He could not place her place in the Professor's scheme of things. Was she merely a tool of the Professor's? Was she a woman whom the Professor loved? Was she—perhaps the brains *behind* the Professor?

To know these things was important, because he must avail himself of every bit of information in the unequal struggle which was to follow. Any fragment, no matter how trivial, might help.

The Professor was now speaking to Wentworth.

"Mr. Spider, you are not as clever as your reputation would have you. Surely, you must have guessed that I would not permit you to come into my presence in the full possession of your faculties?"

Wentworth tried to face toward that voice, trying to locate it exactly. But he could not be sure.

"What do you mean?" he asked.

The Professor laughed. "I mean that you should have prepared yourself better before deciding to allow yourself to be taken prisoner!"

Wentworth barely restrained a gasp of surprise. "How do you know I allowed myself to be captured?"

"Very simple, my dear fellow. From the moment I learned that you were going to visit Jack Blair, I planned every step. I knew very well that it would be useless to attempt to kill you by ordinary means, or to capture you. The men I employ are not clever enough for that. So with the aid of Lona here, I analyzed your character minutely, by studying your former exploits. I arrived at the undeniable conclusion that you would react to certain stimuli. I provided the stimuli, and you reacted as I anticipated. The result is that you are here."

"I see," said Wentworth. "Then you are far more clever than I had anticipated. Far cleverer, my dear Professor, than any criminal I have ever met."

"Thank you, Mr. Spider. That is a compliment, coming from you. But you still do not realize who I am. Do you know why I call myself Professor Secundus?"

"I should be interested to learn," Wentworth returned. "Secundus, of course, means *second*. I am surprised that you should place yourself second to any man."

He said it ironically, knowing the overweening egoism of the average criminal, and hoping to induce the man to continue the conversation until he had located his position in the room with absolute exactitude. But the reply to that thrust of his came like a thunderbolt.

"Second to any *man?*" repeated Secundus. "Ah, no, Mr. Spider. There is no man, living or dead, who can match me. I call myself Secundus because I am the second reincarnation of Evil. *I, my dear Spider, am the new Satan!*"

IT WAS the woman, Lona, who answered. "No, Spider, he is not mad. He has a theory which has worked soundly thus far, the theory of overwhelming the world with such terror that all resistance to Professor Secundus shall be crushed by fear of him. Our campaign has met with nothing but success. Even you—the renowned Spider—" her voice assumed a sharp, spiteful tinge—"stand here, blind and helpless!"

Wentworth was standing on the balls of his feet. Every muscle and fiber in his body was taut. The supreme moment had come.

He said, "Blind, perhaps—*but not helpless!*"

They hadn't searched him. They had fanned him, and taken his two guns. But they hadn't gone through his clothes. This smooth-running, well-oiled organization of the man who called himself the successor to Satan had neglected to strip him of all resources. Did they think then, that the Spider must depend only on his two automatics? In the lining of his cape there was a secret pocket, where nestled a thin, flat little automatic especially made with a clip that held five cartridges. Eighteen caliber only, but it shot hollow-nosed bullets that could do more damage than ordinary bullets fifty percent larger.

It was this gun which the Spider now had in his hand. And just as Professor Secundus was saying in his suave voice edged with mockery, "What do you mean, Spider—'not helpless'—" Wentworth raised the gun and fired five times swiftly, unerringly at the spot where that voice was speaking.

He couldn't miss. He had practiced often, shooting at sounds, and he knew just how to place his bullets in relation to the voice, to strike a mortal spot. As he fired, he expected each split-second, to hear the thunder of answering weapons, to feel bullets smashing into his body. For he was sure that the Professor, or Lona, or both of them, would be covering him while they talked. One of them must surely get him, but he was willing to pay this price for the removal of Professor Secundus.

But no shots answered his own. He emptied the automatic, and he was sure he had not missed. The reverberations of his shots echoed and re-echoed in the small room, so that he could not hear the falling body. He waited until those sounds died away. And then, a deep and awful bitterness welled up within him as he heard, on the heels of the dying gunshot echoes, that same wicked chuckle of amusement which he had heard before, mingled with the tinkling laughter of Lona.

As far as his ears could tell, they were standing in exactly the same spots where they had stood before, and neither of them was harmed. No man could chuckle like that, with even a single wound from a hollow-nosed bullet.

The door behind him opened, there was a rush of feet, and he was seized again.

Sightless, the Spider battled his captors, fighting as perhaps no man has ever fought before against such odds. His hands, reaching, questing for his adversaries, found two men and smashed their heads together with a crack like that of two billiard

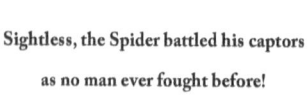

Sightless, the Spider battled his captors
as no man ever fought before!

balls. He lifted another off the floor by a tricky Japanese hold, and hurled the man head-first against the wall.

HIS GREAT and powerful body, trained to the acme of fitness, was like that of some Roman gladiator pitted in the arena against a horde of beasts. He sensed that they were trying to take him alive, to preserve him perhaps for some vile fate which Professor Secundus had planned for him. No knives or guns were evident. But there were blackjacks. By instinct he warded them off as long as he could, not knowing from what direction a blow might descend.

He seized an arm, whirled and heaved, and sent the unfortunate owner hurtling over his shoulder into the mass of the others, uttering a scream of agony. A weighted sap smashed into his right shoulder-blade, almost paralyzing his arm, and another blow struck him at the base of the skull. He went to his knees, with the furious attackers piling on top of him, bearing him down, down.

But with a mighty surge, he heaved up, spinning around and lashing out both fists against bone and flesh. He knew this was the last effort. He could not last longer. There were too many of them for him.

Something struck his forehead, and at the same time another blow landed on his temple. He staggered, but kept on fighting by pure instinct. That great, fighting heart of his refused to give up in spite of blindness, in spite of the hopeless odds.

Reinforcements came into the conflict, and Richard Wentworth was borne down by the sheer weight of numbers. Wire was slipped around his wrists, twisted tight behind his back. Then he was raised to his feet.

"You see, my dear Spider," said Professor Secundus, "that you have been tricked again. You have no chance against me. It is true you are a clever man and a good fighter. But those qualities are not sufficient. I did not forget about searching you. I expected you to do something of the sort you did. Perhaps you understand now why you did not kill me with those well-placed shots?"

"Yes," said the Spider, staring through his unseeing eyes. "I understand. You are somewhere else. You are talking through a microphone, perhaps, connected with a loud speaker."

"Exactly, my dear Spider. Lona and I are behind you, protected by bullet-proof glass. You aimed at the speaker, and it was very good shooting indeed. The speaker was wrecked, and I had to connect another one just now, while you were struggling with my men. But you must admit now, Spider, that you are beaten."

"No," said Wentworth.

"Tut, tut. Will you, at least, listen to my proposition?"

"I'm listening."

"Excellent. The facts are, Mr. Spider, that you are my prisoner, and that you are blind. I offer to set you free and restore your sight."

"How can you do that?" asked Wentworth.

"You were rendered blind by a chemical substance sprayed into the ambulance in the form of a fine powder, which affected the pigmentation of your eyes. As you know, the color of a baby's eyes will change after birth. This is due to the fact that pigment is formed in the human body and coats the iris. My powder stimulates the glands forming pigment, so that they function overtime. The excess pigment blinds you—"

"I understand," Wentworth said quietly, grimly. "I understand now why Doctor Malthus, the famous Vienna eye-surgeon, was kidnapped and later killed, last year!"

"Exactly, my dear Spider!" Professor Secundus said unctuously. "Malthus was kidnapped by my organization. We—er—induced him to reveal to us the secret of this powder. What is more important, we have the formula which he developed as an antidote for the powder. If you recall, Doctor Malthus had stated that he could change the color of anyone's eyes, to order."

"Go on," said Wentworth.

"NOW THEN, my dear Spider, I have discovered by subsequent experimentation that it takes forty-eight hours for the pigment to set. Within those forty-eight hours, if the hypodermic is injected, eyesight may be regained. After that period, however, the subject becomes incurably blind, for that film which is now over your eyes will harden and become indissoluble."

"Well?" said Wentworth.

"I propose," said Professor Secundus, "to set you free, Spider, and give you the hypodermic injection."

"And the price?"

"The price? Merely that you shall become my man. I have great plans, Spider. Within two days the city of New York will be mine—"

"You're mad!" Wentworth interrupted. "Even with this fiendish blindness of yours, you couldn't take over the whole city.

Police Commissioner Kirkpatrick has a trained police force—"

"Tut, tut," Secundus broke
in. "By tomorrow morning the
police force will be working
for *me!* My dear Spider, do you
think I have been laying plans
and building an organization for

one solid year for nothing? Every step is laid out, planned to the
minutest detail—just as your capture. If you could read, I would
show you the latest newspaper extra. It reports the demand I
have made upon Mayor Stanton to dismiss Commissioner Kirkpatrick, and to appoint a man whom *I* shall name!"

Wentworth grunted. "I'm sure," he said ironically, "that Mayor
Stanton will gladly oblige you!"

"He will, Spider, he will. With the pressure that I shall bring
to bear upon him tonight, he will eagerly do what I ask. And
you, Spider, will fit beautifully into my plans. When I take over
the police department, the Underworld must be kept in check,
made to realize that it must take orders from me. *You* shall
be my contact with the Underworld—my *liaison* officer. The
Underworld knows that your word is as good as your bond. You
will promise them loot, and absolute immunity as long as they
acknowledge me as their overlord. Once we control the city,
who knows what may not be next? Perhaps the whole nation.
The threat of blindness is a frightening thing—enough to bring
men in the highest places to their knees."

"How do you know I'd keep my word after I regained my sight?" Wentworth demanded.

Secundus laughed. "I have arranged for that, Spider. Please do not think that I have overlooked the slightest detail. I shall do it in the same way in which I insure the loyalty of my new recruits. I shall give you just enough of the antidote to last for twelve hours. The full antidote, necessary to dissolve permanently the pigment incrustation over your iris, is six drams. I shall give you half a dram every twelve hours. Half a dram will dissolve the pigment, but will not prevent the glands from manufacturing more. If the dose is not repeated each twelve hours, you will go permanently blind. On this basis, you will work for me, doing whatever I require. If you work faithfully, and help me succeed, I shall then give you a full dose of six drams, and you will be permanently cured."

Professor Secundus paused, and a vast, ponderous silence filled the room. Then at last he asked, "Well, Spider? Do you accept?"

"Go to hell!" said Wentworth, and his tone was edged with ice.

CHAPTER 4
SATAN'S DAUGHTER

PROFESSOR SECUNDUS sighed. "I was afraid you would be obstinate. We shall have to try another method with you, Spider."

He raised his voice in harsh order to the men who were holding Wentworth. "Strip the make-up from his face! Let us see who this Spider really is!"

It took half a dozen men to hold him while they scraped the plastic material from his features, removed the wig, and washed the pigment from his face.

And now at last, as he stood once more in the grip of Secundus' satellites, Richard Wentworth knew intense fear—not for himself, but for Nita van Sloan... Nita, his fiancée, the girl who insisted on sharing his life of danger, yet whom he tried always to shelter from danger. It was Nita whom he had sent Ram Singh to guard. But now his fear for Nita mounted and became an ogre before his sightless eyes. For he knew full well what Professor Secundus had in mind.

And Secundus' very next words confirmed that conviction.

But first he heard the voice of the woman, Lona, who had been silent for a long while, so that he thought she had gone away. But now she said in her high, lilting voice, "Ah! He is a very handsome man!"

Professor Secundus disregarded her.

"Now!" he said, and he sounded as if he were rubbing his hands in satisfaction. "Now we are getting somewhere. I seem to know your face. I have seen it in the papers. Let me see, if I recall, you were sitting on a polo pony. *Ah, yes!* You are Richard Wentworth—the well-known sportsman! You are a personal friend of Police Commissioner Kirkpatrick, as well as of Mayor Stanton, are you not?"

Wentworth was silent, his face white and tense, his mind beating against the wall of helplessness to find a way out. Never before had he been thus categorically exposed as the Spider. Commissioner Kirkpatrick, his closest friend, entertained deep suspicions of him, but had never been able to coalesce those suspicions into proof. Often, too, a clever criminal against whom he was pitted had guessed at his identity, But no one had ever before been able to strip the mask from the face of the Spider, and expose Richard Wentworth beneath. It was a testimony to the brilliantly evil mind of Professor Secundus.

The Professor was speaking, and his words crashed through Wentworth's preoccupation.

"You see, Mr. Wentworth, it is my theory that ninety-nine men out of a hundred will break under the threat of lifelong blindness. *You* are the odd one who will not break. For men like you, I have another method. Everyone has some one person whom he cherishes more than anything else in life, for whom he would make every conceivable sacrifice. Surely, you have one such person. I shall soon discover who it is. And then, my dear Wentworth, you will be eager to serve me—"

He was interrupted by the lilting voice of Lona.

"I can tell you what you want to know about him, Professor," she said. "Anyone who follows the society pages would know. The person you want is a young lady—Nita van Sloan."

"Ah, so!" said Professor Secundus. "That is very nice. So very nice!"

He raised his voice, calling out to one of the men who were grouped thickly about Wentworth, as if fearful that he would burst his bonds.

"Cornelius!"

"Yes, sir!"

"Cornelius, take men. Go and investigate this Nita van Sloan. Find out everything about her. But do nothing. Come back and report. I shall—ah—handle the young lady personally. You will report to me at the main headquarters. I am leaving here at once. As for Mr. Wentworth, I am leaving him in your care, Lona, my dear. Have him placed safely downstairs in a cell. Remove everything from his clothing. Leave him nothing which he may use to escape—not even a toothpick. If he offers resistance, chloroform him!"

WENTWORTH'S EARS, rendered more acute by the fact that he could not see, caught the sound of a closing door as Professor Secundus departed. Then, while the tight-pressed group of men continued to hold him, Lona came over and stood in front of him.

"Well, Mr. Wentworth, will you allow yourself to be searched? Or do you prefer chloroform?"

"Go ahead and search," said Wentworth. He had to think, and think clearly now. He must find a way out for himself, blind or not, in order to protect Nita. And he wanted full control of his senses.

Under Lona's expert direction, the men went through his clothing ruthlessly. They took his flat black case of make-up material, and his tool-kit, no larger than a cigarette case, yet which contained precision instruments which had been made to order for him at a cost of eight hundred dollars. They ripped lining, and pulled open the soles of his shoes. They took twenty-five minutes to do the job, and when they were through they had not left him a pin.

The pile of things on the floor excited their curiosity, and they made wondering comments. With the uses of many of the objects they were unfamiliar. There were some things which they were afraid to examine, for they were unacquainted with their nature, and Lona warned them to leave those things alone.

The tool kit excited their especial admiration. With these men, it was professional admiration. For, though many of them were serv-ing the Profes-sor under duress, through the terri-ble fear of blind-ness, there were

many who came from the Underworld. These latter under-stood the uses of the precision instruments which could open any lock, or enable their owner to manipulate the tumblers of any safe in the country.

The true criminals were serving Professor Secundus through greed, and the desire for riches which he had promised them. They began to bicker among themselves for the various objects, especially the tools, until Lona told them sternly that every-thing must be put away, subject to the disposition of Professor Secundus.

Wentworth, standing motionless and unseeing through it all,

marveled at the unquestioning obedience which they accorded the woman.

At her command he was led out of the room and down a flight of steps into a dank cellar. A cell door creaked open, and he was thrust in, with his hands still bound behind him by the wire. But the door was not immediately closed.

He heard Lona say to the men, "All right. You may all go upstairs. Wait for orders by phone from the Professor. You will all be needed at ten o'clock."

Wentworth stood quietly, listening to the receding footsteps of the men. He was aware that Lona had not gone away. As the cellar became silent, he could hear her swift breathing, just outside the cell. Then the scuff of her feet, and she was inside.

He did not move. He was suddenly tense. His nostrils caught the fragrance of a strange, exotic perfume, so delicate that it suggested a single poppy swaying in the breeze. And then she was close to him. Very close. So close that the fabric of her dress over her breasts brushed against his chest. And then he felt long, cool fingertips touching his cheek.

He did not move backward or forward. He stood with his wrists bound behind him, and the wire cutting into them, and waited.

She spoke at last, and her voice was low and throaty now, not high-pitched and lilting as it had been in that other room.

"You love her very much, don't you, Richard Wentworth?" was what she said.

"Yes," he told her.

She did not remove her fingertips from his cheek: "I envy your Nita," she said. "I envy her very much."

Wentworth did not reply in words. He only uttered a short, harsh laugh.

Lona sighed. "I don't think I have ever loved anyone before. I don't think I could love—until I saw you fighting up there. You were blind, and the odds against you were hopeless, yet your courage did not leave you. I never saw a man who dared to defy the Professor. I think that is what made me love you."

WENTWORTH'S LIPS were tight. He tried to make himself believe that this thing was really happening—that the woman who had so callously stood by and aided the Professor, who had pointed out to him the name of the woman whom Wentworth loved—that she was now standing here declaring her own love for him!

Lona was stating wistfully, "I don't suppose you could forget your Nita, could you? You know, I am very beautiful, too. Perhaps not in the same way as Nita van Sloan. I'm much darker than she. But I could make you very happy."

Suddenly she was pressing her body tightly against his, and her arms were around his neck, and she was saying swiftly, "Forget everything, and come in with us, Richard Wentworth! We can go on to unlimited heights of power and glory, and I will make you the most happy man in the world!"

Her body was alive, and warm, and urgent, and she raised herself up against him, and her lips found his with a kiss so passionately abandoned that it burned like something annealed in a white-hot oven.

Of all the things that Wentworth might have expected to happen to him here, this was the last, the most remote from everything possibly conceivable. He let those lips linger while his mind, calm and disassociated, sought to weigh the present situation as being useful or not to his purpose—escape.

At last he backed away. She clung for an instant, and then let her arms drop from around his neck. He could sense her quivering body now as she stepped back, could hear her labored breathing.

At last she gasped, "You—you don't want me, Richard Wentworth?"

"No," he said brutally. "You are a wonderful actress, Lona. Is it necessary to go through all this in order to make an ally of me? Does the Professor need me that badly?"

"Oh!' she cried. And suddenly her hand lashed out and struck him in the face. "You beast!" she said. "Could you think I was acting? Can't you tell I—I—" abruptly she was contrite—"can't you tell I'm in earnest, Richard Wentworth? I—I'm sorry I slapped you. I—I'll do anything for you, Richard Wentworth. Here—I have a hypo with half a dram of antidote in it. I'll give you the injection. You'll see again. You'll see what I look like. Maybe—maybe you'll like me—"

"I'm sorry, Lona," he said. "There is only one woman for me."

"Yes," she sighed. "Yes. I can understand that—now."

Suddenly he felt her long fingers gripping his arm.

"Richard Wentworth," she said urgently, "I'll make a deal with you. I'll give you the hypo, and set you free. Together, we'll go and get the rest of the antidote, enough to cure your blindness completely. In return, you must go away with me. Whether you love me or not, you must do that. Give up your war against the Professor, and he will spare your Nita. But you must never see her again!"

"No," said Wentworth.

"You fool!" she exclaimed. "Don't you understand that this precious Nita of yours will be blind before morning? Don't you want to save her?"

"Yes. To save her, I'd go away with you." He put it as brutally as he could. "But I owe a duty to society. Before I go with you, I must destroy the Professor. Help me to do that, and I'll go with you, and never see Nita van Sloan again!"

"No," she said brokenly. "No. I can't do that."

"Why not? What is the Professor to you?"

For the space of a dozen heartbeats there was utter silence. And then Lona said in a low, almost inaudible voice. "The Professor is—*my father!*"

A terrible, choked sob burst from her throat. He heard her turn around and run headlong out of the cell. Her drumming footsteps died away....

CHAPTER 5
THE DOCTOR WATCHES

A T THAT very moment, Nita van Sloan was sitting stiffly in a chair at the window of her high apartment, overlooking the river.

Her hands were in her lap, and there was a curiously taut

expression in her violet eyes. She sat so straight and tense in the semi-darkness, that one might have thought she was a figure carved in alabaster, were it not for the pulsing beat in her white throat, and the swift rise and fall of her breasts.

Behind her, the bearded Ram Singh was pacing up and down the carpeted floor like a caged cougar.

There was a newspaper on the little end table at Nita's side, and the headline smeared across the page was black and ominous:

SECUNDUS DEMANDS KIRKPATRICK RESIGN OR THREATENS WHOLESALE BLINDNESS IN CITY BY MIDNIGHT!
Two Hundred Twenty Already Stricken Blind. Hospitals Over-crowded. Physicians Helpless!

There was a small, powerful radio on the end table within reach. It was tuned to a station which broadcast frequent news summaries, but at this moment only a low strumming of music emanated from it. Ram Singh kept pacing up and down, between the door at one end of the room, and the window at the other. Whenever he reached the window he would stop and look down into the street, tugging at his full black beard.

But Nita never moved.

The music abruptly died away and a man's voice announced: "We interrupt to bring you an important news bulletin: The mysterious shooting scrape on Second Avenue earlier this evening has developed strange ramifications. The young man who was found, blinded and delirious in the third floor rear flat of tenement house has been identified as Jack Blair, one of the convicts who escaped from State Penitentiary in the early hours of the morning. It is believed Blair could give the answer to the death of three gunmen in that house by an unknown assailant, if he were conscious. The police now reveal that a note found beside Blair proves conclusively that the escaped convict was blinded by Professor Secundus. But there is an added mystery to this case—the question of who killed the three gunmen. From the swiftness with which the unknown killer vanished, police are inclined to believe that the Spider is responsible. A boy states that he saw a cloaked and caped figure resembling the Spider, crossing the yard behind that house, in the company of two other men. Since the Spider is known always to work alone, the boy's story is discounted…."

Nita's hands were clenched in her lap. She did not turn to look at Ram Singh, who had stopped his pacing and was standing at the window.

The announcer hurried on: "Here is another bulletin that just came to the desk: Mayor Andrew Stanton told a press conference tonight that he would definitely not knuckle under to the demand of Professor Secundus that Commissioner Kirkpatrick resign before midnight. The mayor said, quote, 'It is fantastic that a great city should be brought to its knees by one evil man. We shall fight this Professor Secundus with all the resources at our command. I have every confidence in the ability of Commissioner Kirkpatrick, and that confidence is shared by the rest of the city. Kirkpatrick will definitely *not* resign!' unquote. Here is another bulletin on the Blair case: It was established that the gunman, Rolf, who was shot to death by police in the yard behind the Second Avenue house, was not alone down there. He had evidently been lying in ambush behind some trash barrels, accompanied by at least one other man, as the marks in the dust indicate. The other man, or men, escaped through a hole in the fence which they had previously prepared...."

The announcer went off the air, and the music was resumed. **NITA VAN SLOAN'S** breast was heaving. With a quick, impulsive gesture, she shut off the radio and sprang from her chair. She faced the bearded Sikh chauffeur with flashing eyes.

"Ram Singh, you're keeping something from me! Master Dick is in this thing. He was at that Second Avenue house tonight. I knew it when he left me this evening. I knew he was going into something. I suspected it when he insisted on flying back from Miami yesterday."

She took a quick step toward the Sikh. "You've got to tell me, Ram Singh. Is—is he fighting this Professor Secundus? Was it he who killed those gunmen?"

The Sikh bowed his head. *"Missy Sahib,* the Master ordered me not to speak, for fear that you would want to go with him. But I must speak, for I have a great dread upon me now that he is in great trouble. *Missy Sahib,* it is true. The Master went to the Second Avenue house to see Jack Blair. He had given Blair the secret post office box number, where one may write to the Spider for help, which we maintain in the name of Calvin Jones. The letter was automatically forwarded to Florida. Blair wrote that he must see the Spider—so the Spider went to Blair. And now I notice several fellows who are watching this apartment!"

49

THE SPIDER

Nita van Sloan's classically beautiful features were frozen into a mask as she struggled to keep her emotions within control. "Ram Singh! If they are watching us, it—it means—they know that Master Dick is the Spider! For they could associate only Richard Wentworth with me!"

"By *Allah*, it cannot be, *Missy Sahib*. No man could learn whose face lies behind the mask of the Spider, unless—unless—" he broke off biting off his words.

"Say it," Nita exclaimed huskily. "Say what is in your mind, Ram Singh—and in mine! Unless—*unless Master Dick were dead!*"

A low, throaty growl arose, deep in the Sikh's throat. His hand dropped to grip the bone handle of the knife sheathed at his girdle. He threw a glance at the men down in the street.

"I go!" he muttered. "I go to speak with those pigs. If there is aught they know, I shall carve it from their lying hearts!"

Nita put out a hand to restrain him. "Wait—"

She stopped at the gentle, tinkling sound of the muted telephone. There were two phones in the foyer, and at first she uttered a glad cry when she heard the ring. "That's Master Dick—"

But as it rang again, her shoulders drooped. It was not the private phone, by which he would call, but the instrument connected with the foyer below. She shrugged, and went to answer it.

After a moment, she returned, frowning in a puzzled way.

"It's Mrs. Stanton, the mayor's wife," she told Ram Singh.

50

The man seized Mary Stanton. They carried her limp body to the waiting truck.

"She called from the lobby. She's coming up to talk to me. Says it's important."

"Nay, Mistress!" the Sikh growled. "Do not open for her. It is a trick!"

"No, no, Ram Singh," Nita said wearily. "I'm sure it's Mrs. Stanton. I recognized her voice."

"Nevertheless," he insisted, "you shall go in the other room and wait. If it should be a trick—" he showed his two rows of even, white teeth.

Nita complied, walking stiffly, like a somnambulist. *Where is Dick? Where is Dick?* The question kept whirling about in the convolutions of her brain like a funeral refrain.

She picked up a small automatic, which Dick had taught her to use so well, and waited just inside the bedroom doorway while Ram Singh opened the door when the bell rang.

IT WAS no trick, and it was no attack. It was really Bess Stanton, the mayor's wife.

Ram Singh closed and carefully locked the door, and crossed over to the window and stood looking out, with his back to the room, while Nita greeted her, repressing her own worry at sight of the distraught expression upon her visitor's face.

Mrs. Stanton was about forty-five, and extremely good-looking, with gray hair which she made no effort to dye, but which was always perfectly coiffed. Tonight, however, her hair was disarranged, and her lips were trembling.

"Nita," she demanded, "where's Dick Wentworth?"

Nita's eyes widened. "I—I don't know, Bess. Why? Why do you ask?"

The older woman was too nervous to sit down. "I need his help. It's about Mary, our daughter. I'm afraid she's in terrible danger. It's about this—this Professor Secundus. I know Andy and Commissioner Kirkpatrick think highly of Dick Wentworth's ability—and I have no one else to turn to."

Nita put an arm around Mrs. Stanton's waist. She thrust her own worry to the back of her mind, and managed a smile.

"What's the trouble, Bess?"

"Mary is doing a rash thing. She—she got a phone call this evening. It was a man who would not give his name. But he told Mary that if she wanted to get valuable information about Professor Secundus, she was to be at Samson's Grille at nine tonight. And—and she went to keep the appointment. I couldn't stop her. I tried to get hold of Andy or of the Commissioner, but they were out on some important business. And the man who called said that if we communicated with the police it would—would result in many deaths."

"I see," Nita said softly. "So Mary went, alone, hoping to get information that would help to catch this Secundus?"

Bess Stanton nodded, gulping. "And now—I don't know what to do. I dare not call the police after that warning. Perhaps—perhaps you'd go to Samson's Grille with me—"

"Of course!" Nita van Sloan said without hesitation.

She hurried in to the bedroom and came out in a moment with her coat and hat.

"The car is downstairs, Ram Singh?" she asked.

The Sikh protested. "You must not go, Mistress Nita. There

is too much danger. Master Dick said that you should remain at home—"

"That's all out, now, Ram Singh," she said in a flat voice. "Something has happened to Master Dick, and it's up to us to find out what. If Miss Stanton was brave enough to go to that appointment, knowing there was a chance it might be a trap for her, should I remain shut up in here? Besides—" she gestured toward the window—"if those men are really watching us, they'll follow us, and that will prove it. Then perhaps we could turn the tables on them, and make them talk."

The Sikh bowed his head gravely. "So be it, *Missy Sahib,*" he said. They went downstairs with Bess Stanton, and got into the Daimler.

Before they had gone a dozen blocks, they knew that they were being followed. Neither Nita or Ram Singh exchanged a word. Silently, but with a fierce and terrible light in his black and glittering eyes, the bearded Sikh drove uptown.

SAMSON'S GRILLE was one of those new, swank places on Seventh Avenue above Fiftieth Street, with glittering chromium front and glaring neon sign; the bar was ultra-modernistic. When they were a block away, Ram Singh swung the Daimler in to the curb, but did not turn off the ignition. Looking in the rear-vision mirror, he saw that the sedan which had followed them stopped also, double-parking because there was no room at the curb. The sedan remained more than fifty feet behind them. Two men emerged from it, but did not approach. They seemed content to watch.

Mrs. Stanton's nervous fingers were ripping a lace handkerchief to shreds. Her eyes were fixed on the neon sign of Samson's Grille, in the next block.

"I—I wonder if Mary is still there! I wonder if the man kept the appointment—"

"Come, Bess," Nita said firmly. We'll go in there. Ram Singh, you will remain here and cover us, in case those men should follow."

The Sikh did not approve of the arrangement, but he saw the necessity of watching the men who had followed them. He grumbled, but got out of the car with the two women.

"I will walk a little in back of you and Mrs. Stanton," he told Nita. "Do not worry. I will be here!"

The two women started toward Samson's Grille.

It was one minute of nine by a clock in a jeweler's window which they passed.

Bess Stanton stiffened, and pointed. "There! There's Mary, just going into Samson's Grille!"

At the same time, a whistle sounded high and shrill, somewhere down the street. A big truck marked "Furniture," which was parked directly in front of Samson's, began to back-fire with loud, sharp detonations which filled the street, drowning the multitudinous traffic noises.

Nita and Bess Stanton could see Mary Stanton stop short as she was about to enter Samson's. At the same instant, two men came out of the Grille and seized her. She tried to struggle, but one of them hit her in the face and she fell limp. Then they carried her swiftly across the sidewalk to the big furniture truck.

The side door of the truck swung open in perfect timing, and four men with machine guns appeared, covering the dozen or so men who had started to come to Mary Stanton's assistance.

The crowd froze under the threat of those deadly weapons. It was as if all life were standing still on Seventh Avenue, while the two men hustled Mary Stanton's limp body up into the furniture truck. Nobody moved except Ram Singh.

He had caught the significance of the whole action from the very first shrill of that whistle. He had located the man who had blown it, across the street, standing near a lamp post. But he paid no more attention to that man. A huge .45 caliber automatic appeared in his hand, and he leaped past Nita van Sloan and Bess Stanton, racing straight toward the vicious machine-guns in the truck.

"Guard thyself from behind, *Missy Sahib!*" he flung back over his shoulder as his powerful legs pistoned him forward.

But he still had half a block to go. The two men already had pushed Mary Stanton up into the truck. They were climbing in after her, while the gunmen at the door covered them.

Those gunners saw Ram Singh coming and swung their weapons in his direction.

The Sikh was a trained fighting man who had learned every angle of deadly warfare in a hard school. He knew at once that he could never hope to reach that truck in time to save Mary Stanton. It was already moving, and the men at the door were merely going to mow him down before they shut the doors—which were doubtless of sheet steel.

Ram Singh flung himself headlong to the sidewalk under the shelter of a car parked at the curb. He was just in time to avoid the first burst of slugs which whined past him, ricocheting off the face of the building behind the Sikh. Fortunately, no pedestrians were injured. But it was not the fault of the machine gunners. It was only because the passers-by had so hurried to shelter at the first sign of trouble.

Ram Singh leaped around to the other side of the car behind which he had taken shelter, just as a second burst smashed into the radiator. Now the bearded Sikh had the point of vantage he wanted. He leaped up on the back bumper, so that he could see over the top. He thrust out his automatic and sighted along his outstretched arm, pulling the trigger nine times fast.

THE DEADLY slugs from his thundering gun found their mark unerringly. Two of the machine-gunners pitched from the now swiftly-moving truck, landed in the gutter in pools of their own blood. The heavy snub-nosed bullets had literally torn their heads off.

Ram Singh had his second gun out and was ready to fire again, but the remaining two machine-gunners wanted no more of it. They quickly closed the side doors, and the truck sped away, narrowly missing the traffic cop at the corner who had come barging up, gun in fist. The fender grazed him, sent him spinning across the gutter, and the truck was out of sight around the corner.

Ram Singh did not attempt to pursue it. He threw one quick glance over his shoulder and saw that Nita van Sloan was standing with one hand gripping Bess Stanton's arm while she held the small automatic in the other hand, ready for another attack if it should come.

That was all Ram Singh wanted to know. With a shout that was born deep down in his throat he leaped off the bumper and sped across the street to the opposite side, heading straight for a small, wiry man with rat-like features who was rapidly walking away from the lamp post where he had been standing.

The rat-like man saw Ram Singh coming and started to run, but he was looking behind him and not in front; he ran into a hysterical woman. The rat-like man snarled and tried to duck around her, but it was too late. Ram Singh was upon him, and had both hands around his throat.

"Son of a swine!" the Sikh snarled. "It was thou who gave the signal to those killers! With thy whistle!" And he proceeded to throttle the man.

It took three uniformed policemen to drag him off. The rat-like man cowered away from the bearded terror.

"I didn't do a thing!" he whined. "I was just passin'. I ain't no killer—"

A plainclothes detective who had just appeared on the scene shouted, "No crook, eh! That's Willie Hooke. Used to be a finger man for the mobs. Take him in, boys!"

Ram Singh turned and went back to where Nita and Bess Stanton were standing.

"I am sorry, *Sahiba Stanton*," he said contritely. "I am a snail, a slug, a thing of no account. I failed to stop them from carrying off thy daughter."

Mrs. Stanton was leaning heavily on Nita's arm. She closed her eyes hard, and bit her lip, striving to maintain control. Then she said in a tight voice, "No, Ram Singh. You did more than a dozen men could have done. It—it is not your fault."

Then she broke down and buried her head in Nita's shoulder.

"Oh, my daughter!" she sobbed. "Mary! They—they'll blind her!"

There was a wealth of agony in Nita's eyes as she met Ram Singh's glance over Bess Stanton's bowed head. It was all too true. They both knew that Mary Stanton had been abducted for no other purpose. And Nita's gnawing worry about Dick Wentworth clawed at her heart along with this other tragedy.

Ram Singh turned away to avoid her eyes.

He looked for the men who had followed them. But they and their sedan were gone.

"Well," Nita said in a low voice, "there's nothing for us to do but go down to headquarters. Andy Stanton and Commissioner Kirkpatrick will—want to hear about it—after they've questioned that prisoner!"

The Sikh gulped, took Mrs. Stanton's other arm, and they helped her back to the car.

THEY DID not see the limousine which was creeping slowly up the street, nor did they see the tall, gaunt man with deep-set burning eyes, who never took his gaze from Nita van Sloan's trim figure. The limousine was driven by a chauffeur whose face was as noncommittal as the face of the Sphinx. In the interior of this car, a dark and beautiful young woman sat at the side of the gaunt-faced man. She had the mystic, exotic beauty of the orient in her live and quivering features. She, too, was watching Nita van Sloan. But the expression in her eyes was far different

59

from that in the deep-set eyes of the man at her side. Somehow, hers were wistful—one might almost have said, *envious.*

As the limousine passed the crowd gathered around the bodies of the two dead machine-gunners in the middle of the street, a police sergeant looked up and recognized the license plates of the car, which were V-13. He smiled, and touched his cap respectfully. Owing to the jam of traffic the car was crawling so slowly that the police sergeant was able to come alongside and talk to the occupants.

"How are you, Doctor Vendisson?" he asked.

"Very well, thank you, Sergeant Gregg," replied the tall, gaunt man. "Have you met my daughter, Sergeant—Miss Lona Vendisson?"

The dark-haired girl smiled fleetingly at Sergeant Gregg, acknowledged his greeting, then swung her gaze back to where Nita van Sloan was getting into one of the police cars.

"What has been happening here, Gregg?" Doctor Vendisson asked.

"It's that Professor Secundus again, Doctor," the Sergeant told him. "That damned scoundrel's gunmen have carried off Mary Stanton, the mayor's daughter."

Doctor Vendisson raised his eyebrows. "Something must be done to stop this Secundus before he secures control of the city through terror." He glanced down at the sheet-covered bodies of the dead machine-gunners. "Er—who killed these men?"

The sergeant turned and pointed toward the Daimler, which was just pulling away. "See that bearded chap behind the wheel? He's an East Indian of some kind. A Sikh, I guess.

He's the chauffeur for Mr. Richard Wentworth—you know, the Commissioner's friend. Well, that guy is a marvel with a gun. It was he that killed those two babies."

"Ah!" said Doctor Vendisson. "A most interesting person. I do hope, Sergeant, that you have success in catching up with this Professor Secundus."

"Thank you, sir," said Sergeant Gregg.

When the limousine had pulled away, apparently heading in the same direction as the Daimler, Sergeant Gregg turned to a fellow officer who had stood nearby, and said, jerking his head toward the departing limousine, "Great man, that Doctor Vendisson. A wonderful surgeon. He specializes in eye and ear operations. He's working day and night now, trying to figure out a way to cure the people who are being blinded by that devil, Secundus. He's turned over his whole private hospital to caring for them."

"Yeah," said the other officer. "Well, I can't say I like his looks so much. But that's a honey of a daughter he's got. Boy, could I go for her!"

The sergeant's eyes twinkled. "Me, too. That dame has got what it takes!"

"Yeah. I bet she could take her pick of any guy she wanted. I bet nobody would turn his back on *her.*"

"Nope," said Sergeant Gregg. "*Nobody!*"

CHAPTER 6
CAPTURE OF NITA

S ERGEANT GREGG might have hesitated in handing out such unqualified approval of the dark young woman, had he been in a position to overhear the conversation which now took place in the limousine as it followed the Daimler downtown.

"I want her!" said Lona, with a concentrated venom of savage spite which almost transformed her bewitching beauty into a travesty of ugliness. "I want Nita van Sloan. I want her all for myself. When I get through with her, we shall see whether Mr. Richard Wentworth will still love her as much as ever!"

Doctor Vendisson patted her arm. "Tut, tut, Lona, my dear. Haven't I trained you never to allow your emotions to interfere with business?"

She jerked her arm away. "Damn you!"

"Tut, tut," he repeated. "You shouldn't speak that way to your father."

"Father!" she burst out. "You are the Devil! You brought me up to be like this. You made me as evil as you. And now—this man—the only one I have ever met whom I could love—was able to sense the evil in me that you planted from my childhood. You brought me up to hate, to take whatever I wanted, to deny all human sentiments. But you never told me there was such a thing as love. You taught me to laugh at love, and to wind around my finger those men who loved me. But you never taught me what to do when the tables would be turned, and I'd fall in love myself!"

Doctor Vendisson raised his eyebrows. "Do you mean that you are really in love with Wentworth?"

"Yes! I would trade the rest of my life for a year with him!"

Doctor Vendisson shrugged. "Take him then, my dear. We'll keep him under our thumb with the threat of blindness to Nita van Sloan and himself—"

"No!" she said disgustedly. "He won't do it. I—asked him."

Vendisson looked incredulous. "He turned you down?"

"Yes. I literally threw myself at his feet. I offered him his eyesight. But he'd have none of me!"

"H'm," said Vendisson. "Was it because he loves the van Sloan girl?"

"Yes."

"In that case, my dear, I don't blame you for feeling the way you do. You can have her—as soon as I am through with her. I want her for a little while, in order to force Wentworth's hand. You see, I am going to make him—the new Police Commissioner! After I have obtained supreme control of the city, you can have Nita van Sloan."

Lona's eyes were fixed on the car ahead, with a terrible intensity of hatred. "Thank you. I shall make Richard Wentworth come *crawling* to me, to beg for mercy for his sweetheart. And then—" She broke off, pointing ahead. "Look, she's getting out of the car. And they're leaving her behind!"

"H'm," said Vendisson. "This is very nice. So very nice."

He picked up the speaking tube. "Don't follow the Daimler, Eustace," he ordered. "It's the girl we're after."

The car slowed down. Both Vendisson and his daughter watched Nita van Sloan.

What had happened in the Daimler was that Nita had suddenly experienced a terrible feeling of uneasiness. Sitting in the tonneau, with her arm around Mrs. Stanton's shoulders, and watching Ram Singh's broad back, she had suddenly had a feeling that Dick Wentworth was in terrible danger. She had had such premonitions at other times in the past, and they had always been right. Now, the feeling was so strong that she could not bear the thought of going down to headquarters and wasting time there. She had to be doing something—something that might be of service to Dick.

She acted on the spur of the moment. They were passing a restaurant, and the familiar name on the sign caught her eye:

LEGGETTI'S RESTAURANT

Often in the past she and Dick had lunched or dined there. It brought back a rush of memories, and she suddenly felt stifled in the car.

"Stop here, Ram Singh!" she called out.

The Sikh obeyed, wondering.

"I'm getting out," she said. She turned to Mrs. Stanton. "Bess, will you forgive me if I let you go down to headquarters alone? Please try to understand. I shouldn't be leaving you at a time like this. But—but—"

Bess Stanton pressed her hand. "I understand, Nita. It's about Dick that you're worried. Go on. I—I'll be all right."

Ram Singh started to protest, but Nita silenced him peremptorily. "Do as I say!" she ordered. "Take Mrs. Stanton downtown, then come back here. I'll be safe enough. Those men aren't following any more."

The Sikh recognized that tone. When she spoke like that, there was no use arguing with her. He reluctantly opened the door and held it for her.

"I obey, *Missy Sahib*, but I like it not. I shall return quickly. I shall look into the restaurant, and if all is well, I shall remain at the curb with the car till it shall please you to come out."

Nita waited till the Daimler pulled away, then turned and entered Leggetti's Restaurant. She did not see the maroon limousine which pulled up immediately behind her, its occupants observing her closely.

Leggetti's was not busy at this time of evening. Later, when the theatre crowd came out, there would be a jam. Now there were only one or two couples at tables, and no one at the bar.

Nick, the bartender, greeted her with a wide smile. She returned his greeting dully. That premonition of danger to Dick Wentworth was gnawing at her. She went to the phone booth and dialed the number of her apartment.

Her maid answered, and told her no one had called. There was no message of any sort.

Nita sighed. "If—if Mr. Wentworth phones, tell him that I am at Leggetti's. I'll call again in a few minutes, before I leave here."

She hung up, and returned to the bar. She knew now what she

must do. She must go to the place where Dick had last been—to the Second Avenue house. She must take up the trail from there, and follow it to whatever fate lay behind its dark curtain.

She knew, of course, that the police had been all over that ground, but she knew more about the Spider than they did, and she also knew more about the Spider's connection with this case than they did. She might meet success where they had met failure.

She told Nick, the bartender, to give her a coca-cola with just a touch of rum in it; absently, she answered his questions about Wentworth's whereabouts. She did not notice the gaunt man and the darkly beautiful girl who had come in while she was phoning, and were at the bar drinking daiquiris. She did not even glance at the gaunt man when he arose and passed her, on the way to the telephone booths.

Doctor Vendisson entered the booth, and dialed a number. He said, "Cornelius! Ah, good. I see you have already reached headquarters. It was good that you did not remain. The girl has sharp eyes. She knew she was being followed, I believe. Send men now, quickly, to Leggetti's Restaurant. You know where it is? Good. I may not need them, but I wish to have them within call if necessary. You yourself will remain at main headquarters. Have they—er—brought in that other young lady? Excellent. I will attend to her, later. Good-by."

Vendisson left the phone booth with a very benign expression upon his gaunt face. As he passed Nita at the bar, he stopped short, looking at her. He raised his hat and bowed courteously.

"I beg your pardon, miss. But are you not Nita van Sloan?"

Nita glanced up at him, dragging herself away from her concentration of thought upon planning the campaign to trace Dick. She frowned at the interruption, nevertheless she was favorably impressed by this gentleman's careful attire, his impeccable manners.

"Yes," she said. "That is my name."

"Permit me then, to introduce myself. "I am Doctor Arnold Vendisson. I believe that we are both, in a way, interested in the—ah—unpleasant person known as Professor Secundus."

"Oh, yes, I've heard your name often," Nita said, her frown changing to a smile. "You have been devoting all your talent to the problem of solving the Professor's secret of blindness."

"Indeed, yes," he returned. "I believe it my duty to contribute my poor ability in such an emergency. Miss van Sloan, I should like you to meet my daughter, Lona."

He motioned to the darkly beautiful girl, who picked up her drink and came over, with a set smile upon her carmine lips.

"It is a pleasure, I'm sure," Nita said, taking Lona's hand.

The hand was icy cold, and Nita experienced an involuntary, strange shiver as she looked into Lona Vendisson's deep-black eyes. She could not explain it, but she felt a queer antipathy toward this girl, whom she was sure she had never met before, and whose path she was sure could never have crossed hers.

"I have heard so much about you, Miss van Sloan," Lona Vendisson purred. "Your picture appears so often in the Society pages, with that of your fiancé, Richard Wentworth."

Nita laughed a little. "I'm afraid there won't be much society news until—until—" she almost said: *until I find Dick again,* but she changed it to—"until Professor Secundus has been destroyed."

"Quite so," said Lona. She kept looking at Nita. "You know," she exclaimed suddenly, "you are very beautiful, Miss van Sloan."

"Thank you," said Nita. "You flatter me. It is you who are very beautiful, Miss Vendisson. I hear that you are also very learned. They say that you assist your father very ably at his hospital."

Lona shrugged. She threw a quick side-glance at Vendisson. "My father," she murmured, "has trained me well. Very well."

Nita was uncomfortable under Lona's constant, searching glance. Almost, Nita thought, it was as if the other girl were calmly dissecting her, like a specimen under glass.

The doctor plunged into a lengthy, technical discussion of the conformation of the eye, advancing it as his theory that the curious blindness was connected in some way with the pituitary gland.

"If that should be so," he explained, "there is little hope for the victims of Professor Secundus, because the pigment which is formed over the iris hardens in such a way that after twelve hours there would be no means of removing or dissolving it."

"Have you attempted to remove it within the twelve hours?" Nita asked.

"Yes, indeed. But I have discovered no substance—no antidote—which will do it. And operation in these cases, is out of the question. Even I would not dare to attempt such an operation."

They continued to discuss the subject, with Lona taking very little part. Nita wondered why Doctor Vendisson was going to such lengths to explain the technical side of the mystery to her, but she was glad to listen to anything at all which might cast additional light on the subject, or which might, by the farthest stretch of the imagination, furnish her with a clue as to where to look for Dick. She noticed that the doctor had a curious nervous habit of twitching his head as if to look out the window at frequent intervals, but she ascribed it to the high tension under which he was living these days.

"Perhaps," he said finally, "you would be interested in visiting my hospital? You may wish to talk to some of these unfortunates who have been blinded. Especially, that young man—what's his name—" he frowned as if with an effort of memory, and turned to Lona, who supplied it.

"You mean Jack Blair, father?"

"Ah, yes. That's it. Jack Blair. The young escaped convict, who was blinded this evening. We hope he will recover consciousness soon, and be able to talk."

Nita restrained the sudden eagerness she felt. There was the logical place to start. If Jack Blair could talk, he might be able to tell her what had happened to the Spider!

"Why, yes," she said, endeavoring to make her voice sound casual. "I should love to come. It's very kind of you to ask me."

"Then we can go at once!" Doctor Vendisson exclaimed. "In fact, we were on our way to the hospital when Lona suggested a moment's relaxation."

"If you could only wait a few minutes," Nita asked. "I'm expecting Mr. Wentworth's chauffeur to return for me. He— he took poor Mrs. Stanton down to headquarters."

Vendisson glanced at his watch. "It is growing rather late. I should really be starting for the hospital. Couldn't you—er—leave word here for your chauffeur to follow to the hospital when he comes?"

Nita nodded. "I'll do that." She called Nick over. "When Ram Singh comes, will you tell him I've gone to Doctor Vendisson's hospital? Tell him to call for me there."

"Sure thing, Miss van Sloan," Nick grinned.

"If you will excuse me," Nita said to Vendisson, "I want to phone my apartment—in case there have been any calls."

She entered the phone booth once more, leaving the door open, and dialed her own number.

"Any calls, Susanne?" she asked eagerly.

"No, miss. None at all."

"If Mr. Wentworth should call," she told the maid, "ask him to call me at once at the Vendisson Eye and Ear Hospital. Better still, ask him to go straight over there. I'll phone you again before I leave the hospital."

When she emerged from the booth, Doctor Vendisson had paid for the drinks. He took Lona and Nita each by an elbow, and led them out to his limousine in a fatherly way.

He helped them into the car while Eustace, the chauffeur, stiffly held the door open. Then he said, "Ah, I think I know that man. Excuse me for just a moment."

He stepped away from the car and spoke to a man who happened to be standing a few feet away.

"Cornelius," he said, speaking very low, "I want you to remain here. Soon, that Sikh chauffeur of Wentworth's will drive up in

70

the Daimler. Dispose your men in such a way as to intercept the car before it reaches Leggetti's. Capture the Sikh, if possible. If it is not possible to capture him, kill him. Then you will kill the bartender in Leggetti's. You will also send men to Miss van Sloan's apartment, and kill the maid. I wish that no one should remain alive with the knowledge that Miss van Sloan is going to the hospital with me."

Cornelius was a round-faced man, with ruddy cheeks and innocent-looking blue eyes, and an expression which might cause one to believe that he was a pious, church-fearing citizen. In reality he was a cruel killer who took human life without the least compunction.

"Right, Boss," he said, with a cruel gleam in his light-blue eyes.

Vendisson hurried back to the limousine, and climbed in, seating himself between Nita and Lona.

"Strange how one meets former patients everywhere," he murmured. "I operated on that man's eyes five years ago."

Eustace got behind the wheel. The doctor picked up the speaking-tube and said, "Straight to the hospital, Eustace."

He leaned back as the car swung away from the curb, and looked sideways at Nita. "It is very nice that you are coming to the hospital. So very nice!"

"Yes," said Lona, with a queer lilting tone in her voice. "I'm *sure* it will be very nice!"

71

CHAPTER 7
THE SPIDER RETURNS

RICHARD WENTWORTH did not know how long he stood motionless in his cell, after Lona left him, her heels drumming a swift retreat upon the floor.

Though he could not see, he knew that she had left the cell door open. He knew also, that he had thrown away a chance at freedom, a chance at regaining his sight—because he could not deceive a woman.

How easy it would have been to say, "Yes, Lona, I love you. Yes, I will forget the Professor, give up my crusade against him, and go away with you, and forget Nita!" How easy—and yet, how impossible for Dick Wentworth.

She had had that hypodermic with her. With one word, he could have regained his eyesight—for only twelve hours. But what a difference twelve hours would have made!

Now, he could expect nothing from Lona but hate—hate and fury of a woman scorned. And that hate of hers would seek its outlet against Nita.

Wentworth closed his sightless eyes, hard. He must think, think. He could walk out of the cell now, of course. But there must be men in this building—whatever it was. There would be passages to traverse, doors to open, fights to fight. He must do all this blindly, and if he failed, Nita would pay the price.

Suddenly, a muscle in his throat contracted. His bound hands tautened behind him, and his brain whirled with the thought which had just come into it.

He forced himself to stand utterly still, so that he could think clearly. He sent his mind back over every little detail of those short few minutes during which Lona had been in the cell.

She had stood outside, in silence. She had come in, she had stood here, close to him. She had talked. She had said that she had the hypodermic with her.

Yet when she put her arms around him she had clasped her hands behind his neck.

And there had been nothing in her hands!

He forced himself to remain dispassionate, analyzing the situation as if it did not concern him, just as if it were an academic problem. There were two possibilities: Either she had lied to him about having the hypodermic, or she had not lied. If she had lied, then the whole thing had been an act. But only a consummate actress could have made passion seem so real. Then if she had not lied, she must have put the hypodermic down somewhere—either in the corridor or in the cell.

Tensely, not daring to hope, Wentworth stepped forward, feeling each step carefully. He reached the door, and it was open. He stepped through, shuffling his feet, lest, if the hypo be on the floor, he should crush it.

His feet encountered nothing. He felt around, first to one side, then to the other, moving with infinite caution, inch by inch.

And he touched something—something light.

Swiftly he got down to his knees, then sat on the floor and turned around with his back to the object, so that his bound hands could touch.

73

A surge of elation swept through him as his questing fingers encountered the plunger of the hypodermic!

Gently he lifted it up, felt along it until he touched the needle, to make sure it was not broken. Then, holding it carefully, he maneuvered to his feet again. He held the hypo in his right hand. But his wrists were bound so tightly that it was impossible for him to administer the dose of sight-giving fluid into his arm.

The house dissolved into a million flying fragments.

There was no antiseptic, but he didn't care. All he wanted was to see again for twelve hours. After that, let happen what might.

He bent over toward the right, held the plunger skillfully with his thumb over the top, and slipped the needle into his thigh. He drove the plunger home.

With a sigh, he straightened. He stood and waited. FAINTLY, ABOVE, he could hear men walking. From somewhere he heard the noise of a railroad train. There was a little quick scurry as a mouse scampered past him. He waited, with his eyes closed. He counted a hundred, two hundred, then went on… two hundred and one, two hundred and two….

He didn't want to open his eyes. He didn't know how long it would take the antidote to work. He thought he could feel excessive moisture in his eyeballs, but it might be only imagination, wishful thinking. He reached three hundred, and though his eyes were still closed, he was conscious of *light.*

He exhaled a deep, long breath, and opened his eyes.

He could see!

He was in a corridor, part of a basement. At the far end of the corridor, there was the open space devoted to heating equipment. There were two barred windows far overhead, and they were shuttered from the outside. The sole illumination came from a bulb overhead.

The cell from which Wentworth had emerged was one of two such cells in the corridor. The other one was unoccupied.

He looked around, studying his surroundings, but could get no hint as to what sort of building he was in. His eyes smarted a little, but he could see as well as ever. The antidote had completely dissolved the pigment which had formed over the irises of his eyes, but he knew that the glands would be forming more. Twelve hours. Twelve hours of blessed eyesight, in which to pit his energies and his wits in a supreme battle against the man who called himself the reincarnation of Satan. Then, blindness again.

Wentworth's jaw was hard. He glanced down the corridor to the staircase which led up to a door that was closed. On that upper floor, he could hear men walking. Up there lay battle. And it was the way for him.

He began to search for some sharp projection against which he could chafe the wire. Suddenly he stiffened. *Someone was opening the door at the head of the stairs!* He turned and darted back down the corridor into the boiler room. He saw the door up at the head of the stairs open slowly, almost stealthily. And Eric appeared.

Eric was holding a gun, and he was tense, crouching. He was looking behind him, and backing down the stairs as he closed the door. He came down the stairs silently, throwing frequent glances over his shoulder. He approached the cell which Wentworth had just vacated, and peered in, frowning against the darkness, seeing the door of the cell swinging open.

"P-st!" he whispered. "Spider! Are you in there?"

"No," said Wentworth. "Here I am."

Eric whirled as if he had been shot. And then he came running over.

"Spider! I came to get you out of here. You've got to help me!"

"All right," said Wentworth. "Get this wire off my wrists."

ERIC'S FUMBLING fingers untwisted the wire, and it fell away. Eric took a gun out of his pocket and thrust it into Wentworth's hands. He also took out a hypodermic syringe.

"I—I brought this for you. I stole it from Manson's locker."

"Who is Manson?" Wentworth asked.

"He's in charge here when the Professor is gone. I—I thought you were still blind. What—what happened?"

Wentworth laughed grimly. "I got a break." He inspected the hypo Eric was holding. "How come Manson had one of these?"

"They use them every twelve hours. Most of the men working for the Professor are like me—they have to get a dose at regular intervals. When they come in, Manson gives them the hypo full, then waits for the Professor to bring more. The professor doesn't keep more than two drams in the place at one time, so no one can get a full cure."

"I see," said Wentworth. "What sort of place are we in?"

"God help me, I don't know. They don't trust me, yet. They never let me down here. I had to sneak down. And every time I come here, or to the main headquarters, it's in a closed truck or ambulance, and they blind me before coming in, just the way they did tonight. Then they give me a hypo full, and I can see again—for twelve hours. But I've never seen the outside of this place. The windows are all shuttered, and the doors are barred. A man with a rifle stands guard at the front door, all the time."

Wentworth broke the gun Eric had given him, made sure all the chambers were loaded.

"Why do you want me to help you?" he asked.

Eric's eyes were half-mad. "I'm all done here. I got into it because I was mad about that girl—Lona. At first I didn't know what it was all about. Then, when they asked me to do something I didn't like, they gave me a taste of the blindness. I'd have kept on anyway, I guess, because I'd have done anything Lona asked. But yesterday she told me she had no use for me. So—so I'm through."

"H'm!" mused Wentworth. "She must be very beautiful, this Lona."

"Beautiful? That's no word for it. She—she makes you feel you're just walking on air, looking at her. I'd die happy if—if she would be mine for one night!"

Wentworth wasn't listening very closely. He had noted a neat pile of boxes in a dark corner of the cellar, at the far end, beyond the boiler. He was frowning, peering at them. He left Eric standing there, and went over to the boxes. There were four of them. Out of each box a wire ran through a carefully set outlet, up to meet the others, then they were all taped together into a single line which led up along the wall and through a tiny aperture in the ceiling of the cellar. Wentworth thoughtfully felt the boxes, then came back into the corridor.

"Tell me, Eric," he asked. "Why would there be four boxes of dynamite down here, all wired together?"

"Dynamite?" Erie looked puzzled, then exclaimed. "That's it, of course! The Professor has told us often that this place, as well as the main headquarters, is mined in case it should ever be raided. The whole place would be blown up, together with the raiding party. He says that's why he doesn't want us to go out on the grounds. Because there's a detonator out there which will set it off as we escape."

"All right, Wentworth said tightly. "Let's go."

He started for the stairs, and Eric grasped his sleeve.

"What are you going to do?"

"What am I going to do?" Wentworth laughed harshly. "I'm going to shoot my way out of here. Are you with me?"

"Yes!"

"Then come on!"

He mounted the stairs, stood for a second with his hand on the knob, hearing Eric's labored breathing behind him.

Then he pushed the door open and stepped through. Eric crowded close at his heels.

THEY WERE at the rear of a long hall, with doors on both sides. At the front of the hall there were three short steps down to the foyer, with a barred steel door closing off egress. Sitting alongside the door was a guard who was peering out through a peephole.

The guard turned at the sound of the opening door, at first not suspecting anything until he saw Wentworth. Then he uttered a hoarse exclamation and raised the rifle. Wentworth shot him through the heart.

The man uttered a hoarse, stifled yell, and fell over the long barrel of his gun.

Wentworth raced forward, stooped and picked up the rifle. He thrust Eric at the door, saying, "Unbar it. I'll hold the others back!"

Eric worked with desperate fingers. He raised the bar, hurled it to one side, and then stooped to find the guard's keys in order to open the lock.

Meanwhile, Wentworth faced the hall, with the rifle in front of him. Men were shouting inside, and one of them appeared in the doorway of a room down the hall. The man had a gun in his hand, and when he saw the guard on the floor he dropped to one knee and tried to shoot at Wentworth from behind the door jamb.

Wentworth grimly raised the rifle to his shoulder and fired, all in a single swift motion. He was, if anything, more accurate with a rifle than with a revolver. He hit the half-inch of exposed face, and the man disappeared. Others began coming out fast now, and Wentworth kept pumping his rifle until it was empty. Then he threw it down and took out the revolver once more.

But he had no need to shoot again, for the remaining gunmen were not risking a slug from that uncannily accurate marksman.

Eric yelled, "Okay! It's open!"

Wentworth nodded, and started backing out. From the corner of his eye he saw that Eric was doing something swiftly, at a small switch-box just inside the doorway, but he had no time to waste, for the gunmen inside were getting up courage for another rush. He fired three times fast to discourage them, then leaped out into the open. It was pitch-black out here, and he bumped into Eric who grasped his arm and yelled, "Quick! Let's get away from here!"

Eric had hold of his arm, and dragged him away.

"Wait," said Wentworth. "I want to make sure they don't come after us—"

"Never mind, never mind!" Eric babbled. "Come on."

A figure appeared in the doorway, and Eric fired, emptying his gun. The figure swayed, and fell inward.

"That's right!" said Eric. "Stay in there, damn you!"

He turned to run again. "Come on, Spider," he shouted. *"Come on, if you want to live!"*

"What do you mean?" Wentworth asked suspiciously, running at his side, keeping a watch over his shoulder for pursuit.

"You'll see, you'll see in a minute. I pulled the detonator switch for the dynamite just before we went out. I opened the box with the guard's keys. They don't know about it yet, in there. It's timed to go off in three minutes, to give everybody in there a chance to leave—"

His words were drowned by a flashing *boom* like the collision of two flaming meteors. The earth rumbled under their feet, and the house they had just left seemed to dissolve into a million flying bits of metal, wood, and fire. The sky was streaked with the flame of the explosion, and the detonation beat against the eardrums with deafening force. Fragments of the building began to rain down upon them like flying shrapnel.

Wentworth grabbed Eric and started to drag him down, and then he felt Eric jerk in his grip. A bit of steel, eight or nine inches long, had struck him in the temple, and was buried almost halfway.

It quivered with the vibration of its flight. There was no blood. Eric stiffened, his face became a frozen mask, and his eyes assumed a queer, opaque look. Then he fell over, dead.

Wentworth wasted no pity on him. He had been willing

to do anything to satisfy his desire for a woman. He had only decided to quit when he could not get that woman. And he had perhaps hoped that the Spider would find a way to spare him from blindness when the twelve hours were up.

Richard Wentworth turned and walked away.

THE HOUSE had been set on a hill, by itself, with a long view of the Hudson River and the Palisades. It was far above the city, and it would be a long trek back. Wentworth had no money in his pockets. He would have to beg a lift, get to one of his furnished rooms where he kept changes of clothing, reserve money and reserve weapons. Then he must resume the deadly battle with Professor Secundus. He must find Nita, arrange to protect her day and night against harm—if it was not already too late. And lastly—he must, within twelve hours, break the secret of Professor Secundus' antidote to the glandular pigment. Else he would soon become blind once more—this time, forever.

He discarded the cloak which tagged him as the Spider, and worked his way down to Riverside Drive before the fire engines and the police arrived at the burning building. It was a long time, however, before any motorist stopped to give him a lift. It took him almost a half hour to get to downtown New York.

Wentworth went to his nearest retreat and immediately phoned Nita's apartment. There was no answer. His heart began to beat faster. It could mean only one thing. Secundus had already struck.

His fingers flew as he changed to fresh clothing, and equipped himself with automatics, fresh clips, make-up material, and a thin Spider cape made of rubber, which fitted into a special pocket. While he worked, he turned on the radio. He caught a special news broadcast—not unusual, with the terror of Professor Secundus upon the city.

From the broadcast he learned of the kidnapping of Mary Stanton, and he understood what Secundus had meant when he said that he would soon exert pressure upon Stanton to choose a new Police Commissioner. He heard the details of the fight between Ram Singh and the gunmen, and learned that Nita, Bess Stanton and Ram Singh had started down for headquarters.

That was all he wanted to know. He picked up the phone, dialed headquarters, and got Commissioner Kirkpatrick.

"Dick!" exclaimed the Commissioner. "Where have you been all evening? God, I've been asking for you everywhere. Ram Singh is insanely worried about you. I don't know why. Can't get him to tell me what it's about."

Wentworth smiled grimly. It would be interesting to see Kirkpatrick's expression if the Sikh were suddenly to say, "My master is the Spider. He went to seek Secundus, and he has not returned. Please look for the Spider!"

No, the Spider worked alone, without benefit of the law, and took the risks that went with such a method of operation. The Spider himself was outside the law, and would be clapped in jail as quickly as Professor Secundus—if captured. And no matter how close Kirkpatrick's friendship with Wentworth, once he obtained the proof to link Dick with the Spider, the Commissioner would do his duty as he saw it, even though it would break his heart to send his best friend to the chair.

So Wentworth merely said, "Have you any clues to the location of Professor Secundus' headquarters? Have you been able to make this Willie Hooke talk?"

"No, damn it! We've given him everything in the house. We've third-degreed him to a fare-thee-well. But he's apparently in greater terror of Secundus than he is of us. What in the world kind of hold can Secundus have on these guys, that he makes them do murder and worse?"

"Listen, Kirk," Wentworth said earnestly. "Suppose something was done to you, so that you would become blind in twelve hours unless Secundus gave you an antidote. Would you obey him to the bitter end in order to save yourself from blindness?"

At the other end he heard Kirkpatrick suck in his breath, sharply. "Dick," he asked in a hushed voice, "are you *sure* of this?"

"Sure," said Wentworth. "Absolutely sure."

"Dick," said the Commissioner, "if we could get a sample of this antidote, it would save the city!"

Wentworth said slowly, "Kirk, I have half a dram of it."

"*What?*"

"I have a hypodermic with half a dram of the antidote. Don't ask me how I got it. Take my word for it that it works. I'm bringing it right down. You can have it analyzed in the police laboratory, and start manufacturing it in quantity. We'll feed it to the victims of Professor Secundus who are in Vendisson's Eye and Ear Hospital, and when the news is published that we can cure the blindness, all the unwilling slaves of Professor Secundus will desert him."

"Bring it down, Dick, bring it down!" Kirkpatrick exclaimed.

"Dick, did the Spider have anything to do with getting that sample?"

"I don't know what you're talking about, Kirk. I'll be right down. But first, will you let me talk to Nita?"

"Nita isn't here, Dick. Ram Singh is here. He tells me that Nita stopped off somewhere on the way downtown."

WENTWORTH'S GRIP tightened on the phone. "Let me talk to Ram Singh!" he said hoarsely.

In a moment the Sikh was on the wire.

"Master!" he exclaimed in Punjabi. "I had lost hope of seeing you in this world. I—"

"Ram Singh!" Wentworth interrupted. *"Where is Nita?"*

"Master," the Sikh said miserably, "I could do naught with her. She insisted upon visiting Leggetti's. She ordered me to return there for her. And now the pig of a District Attorney refuses to permit me to leave until I have furnished bond that I shall return to swear testimony against that pig of a Willie Hooke whom I caught. Thus do they reward men who fight the battles of the police for them. It seems that I am now a *material witness*, and I may not leave without posting bond!"

"All right, Ram Singh. I'm coming down. I'll stop off at Leggetti's and pick Nita up. Don't worry, old friend, I know you can do nothing when she gets one of her moods."

He hung up, and called Leggetti's. "Nick?" he asked.

"This ain't Nick," an Irish voice told him. "Who's this?"

"Richard Wentworth calling."

"Ah, Mr. Wentworth! This is Patrolman McGuire. A terrible thing just happened. Couple hold-up men opened up with machine guns on poor Nick. He's dead and they got clean away."

"I see," said Wentworth, in a low voice. He knew Nick Piombo very well. Nick had been supporting a boy in college, and a daughter who was taking singing lessons. Wentworth made a mental note to create a trust fund to carry the boy and the girl along.

"Mac," he asked, "is Miss van Sloan there?"

"No, sir. Not a sign of her."

"She—she wasn't carried off by those gunmen?"

"Heaven bless me, no sir. They got away by themselves, without taking a soul. There's several witnesses saw them. Nobody was snatched. They just killed Nick, and scrammed. Looks like that's all they came to do."

Wentworth hung up, his eyes bleak. He was sure that there was some sort of connection between Nita's presence in Leggetti's, and the death of Nick Piombo. If Nita had departed before the shooting, why had Nick been killed? To shut his mouth? Had poor Nick seen something he hadn't been supposed to see?

Wentworth wanted urgently to go there and look around for himself, to get some lead to where Nita had vanished. But there was something even more urgent—the analysis of the half-dram of antidote which he had gotten from Eric. The eyesight of more than two hundred victims in Vendisson's Eye and Ear Hospital depended on getting that antidote within twenty-four hours. Grimly, he remembered that his own eyesight, too, depended upon it. The others, though, needed it more urgently than he. Wentworth had almost eleven hours more to go....

CHAPTER 8
BARGAIN WITH DEATH

O N THE way downtown in the taxi-cab, Wentworth received another jolt when he turned on the radio and heard the tail of another news flash: "… unexplained raid by gunmen upon Miss Nita van Sloan's apartment. The only victim of the attack was Susanne LeClerc, a maid employed by Miss Nita van Sloan, beautiful social registerite. Miss van Sloan was not at home at the time, and could not be located for an interview. This murder, following upon the heels of the cold-blooded machine-gunning of Nick Piombo, a bartender at Leggetti's, can only be explained as the work of the sinister figure who calls himself Professor Secundus, and who straddles the city now, a Colossus of Crime…."

Wentworth stared straight ahead, rigid with thought, as the cab rolled southward. First Nick, then Susanne. Death was striking relentlessly at those who were in any way associated with the Spider, or who came in contact with him. What had these two innocents done to deserve such a fate? It had been their misfortune to know something about Nita van Sloan—something that would have pointed to a guilty person, or to a secret which must be kept at any price. But how to find that person or that secret? How to reach the vicious fiend who called himself the reincarnation of Satan? How to punish him? How to insure for all time that he would not be a menace to mankind?

These things the Spider must do—and he must do them quickly, before eleven more hours passed, else the Spider would once more be blind and helpless against the most redoubtable adversary he had ever faced.

Another news item came blaring from the radio: "A mysterious explosion was reported from the Riverdale section of the Bronx. The cause of the explosion is unknown, but police believe it to have been caused by a cache of dynamite in the basement of a building which housed a private school for male nurses. All in the building died. There are no survivors. The entire structure was burned to the ground after the explosion, and the charred bodies are being removed. No reason has been assigned for the presence of the dynamite…."

When the cab reached headquarters, Wentworth hurried inside. He was so preoccupied in piecing together in his mind all the evidence he had gathered during the evening, that he did not notice the man who was sitting in the parked sedan across the street.

This man had a round, ruddy face, and a pair of light-blue, innocent-looking eyes. But they were eyes which had only a little while ago looked without twinge at the riddled body of Nick Piombo, and the pitiful dead body of Susanne LeClerc.

Now, those light-blue eyes looked with startled wonder at the broad back of Richard Wentworth, which was disappearing into the headquarters building.

The man got quickly out of the sedan, and hurried to a corner phone. He inserted a nickel, and dialed a number.

"Boss," he said, "this is Cornelius."

"Ah, yes, Cornelius. You have done very nicely so far, with those other two matters. But what about the—er—chauffeur?"

"He's still in police headquarters, Boss. I got the boys planted at both ends of the street, so they can get him either way he goes. But listen, Boss—I just seen a ghost!"

"What do you mean?"

"I just seen Wentworth walk into headquarters. And nobody was leading him, either. Boss, *he could see!*"

"Impossible, Cornelius. In the first place, it is a physical impossibility to see again without a hypo. In the second place, everybody perished up there in the explosion. He was in a cell—"

"Boss, I saw him with my own eyes."

There was a pause. Then, "All right, Cornelius. I'll check on it."

"You want this guy taken care of?"

"No, no. If what you say is true, I am very glad to hear it. He will be very valuable to me, Cornelius. Very valuable."

Cornelius grinned. He hung up and went back to his sedan.

INSIDE HEADQUARTERS, Wentworth hurried to the chemical laboratory, where Kirkpatrick was already awaiting him. The Commissioner took the wrapped-up hypodermic almost reverently, and handed it to Doctor Nelson, the Chief Chemist.

"You know what to do with this?"

Nelson nodded. "I'll go right to work on it."

"And for God's sake," Wentworth cautioned, "don't use any more of it than you can help. There's enough in there to save some person's eyesight for twelve more hours!"

They left the lab, and went quickly upstairs to Kirkpatrick's office.

"I'm not asking you where you got that, Dick," the Commissioner said. "I'm not asking you any questions. At a time like this I'd accept help from the devil himself. And if the Spider wants to work with me on this, why—" he gulped, for it was a tremendous concession for him to make—"why, by God, I'll work with the Spider!"

"I'm sure," Wentworth said smoothly, "that the Spider would be glad to hear you say that."

"The trouble is," Kirkpatrick said bitterly, "that I may not be Commissioner much longer. We can't get Willie Hooke to talk. Stanton pins his hopes on finding from Hooke where his daughter was taken, and staging a raid. But if Hooke keeps his mouth shut Stanton will weaken. He won't let his daughter be blinded. He'll knuckle under, and ask for my resignation, and put in some one whom Secundus names. And I can't say that I'd blame him much—not when it means saving pretty little Mary Stanton from a lifetime of blindness!"

Wentworth's lips were tight. He was thinking of Nita. Was she in the same place as Mary Stanton now? Would she be blind the next time he saw her? Or *would* he see her? Within less than eleven hours he, too, would become totally blind.

In Kirkpatrick's office, Mayor Stanton and big, husky Inspector MacGowan were questioning Willie Hooke. Hooke was snarling defiance. He had the face of a rat, and the soul of a beast at bay. He talked with a nasal whine, and his voice was high and sharp.

"I don't know a thing, see? I was just passin' when that crazy coot wit' the beard grabbed me. I don't know a thing about no Mary Stanton. Never seen her in my life."

LONA VENDISSON

Mayor Stanton, tall with graying hair at the temples, was standing rigid in the middle of the room, his eyes ever on Willie Hooke. It was obvious that he was making every effort to hold himself together. He turned when the door opened, and tendered Wentworth a weary greeting. He gestured toward Hooke.

"This rat sticks to his story. And in the meantime they—they may be—blinding my Mary!"

Kirkpatrick waved to Inspector MacGowan. "Take Hooke away and book him."

MacGowan dragged the little man out of the room, and Kirkpatrick locked the door. Then he turned to Wentworth and Stanton. He put a hand on Mayor Stanton's shoulder.

DR. VENDISSON

"It's no use, Andy. You can't sacrifice your daughter. No city can ask that much of a man—mayor or no mayor. I'll give you my resignation. You can announce it in the papers, so Secundus will know. At least that may save Mary—for a time."

Stanton bowed his head wearily. "My wife is downstairs in the matron's room," he whispered. "She'll—die if—if Mary should be blinded. I'd lose my whole family at a single stroke. I can't hold out any longer, Kirk. I'll have to do it."

The phone rang, and Kirkpatrick picked it up, listened for a moment, then handed it to Wentworth.

"For you, Dick."

Wentworth stiffened as he heard the same suave voice of Secundus.

"Congratulations, Mr. Wentworth, on your happy escape. I congratulate you also upon regaining your eyesight. My daughter tells me she must have left a single hypo, with half a dram of the serum. You know, of course, that you will be blind again by tomorrow morning?"

WENTWORTH FELT a wave of cold anger hit him. How had Secundus learned so quickly that he was down here in headquarters?

He motioned swiftly to Kirkpatrick to trace the call. Then he said coldly into the instrument, "Who is this talking? I don't know what you're talking about!"

There was a pause, then the voice of Professor Secundus came once more. "Am I talking to Mr. *Richard* Wentworth?"

"Yes, of course. This is Richard Wentworth. But what do you

mean about recovering my eyesight? And what is this about your daughter? Who are you?"

"Please do not make things difficult," the voice snapped. "This is Professor Secundus speaking. I warn you not to attempt to trace this call, or it will result fatally for Miss Stanton, the mayor's daughter."

Wentworth had been holding the receiver a little away from his ear, so that Kirkpatrick and Stanton could hear the man at the other end. Now, as Stanton heard that warning, he grasped the arm of Kirkpatrick, who had jumped to the inter-office phone to put through an order to trace the call.

"No, no!" Stanton whispered. "They'll finish Mary. Let's deal with him!"

Kirkpatrick shrugged, and did not put through the order.

Wentworth continued his bluff. "Very well, you have my word for it that the call is not being traced. But please explain what you mean about my blindness. You seem to think I have been in contact with you."

He pressed the receiver close to his ear, so that the Commissioner and the Mayor could not hear the reply, and he was glad he had done so, for Secundus barked, "Wentworth, do not trifle with me. You, as the Spider, were my prisoner two hours ago. Somehow, you managed to escape. Just now you were seen entering headquarters—"

"My dear Professor," Wentworth drawled, subtly changing his voice so that it would not sound familiar to the other, "I am afraid you are laboring under a misapprehension. What you say is utterly ridiculous. What is your purpose in making this call?"

95

Secundus chuckled. "Have it your way, Wentworth. Since you claim you are not the Spider, you were never my prisoner. Since you were never my prisoner, you were never blinded. Therefore you will not need any further doses of the antidote. Now, what do you say?"

"I still say that I don't know what you're talking about."

"Very well then. Perhaps you will understand this—*I want a contribution of one hundred thousand dollars from you, immediately after the banks open tomorrow morning!*"

"Are you crazy," Wentworth demanded. "Why should I pay you a hundred thousand dollars?"

"Because if you don't—a very dear friend of yours will never be able to see again!"

Wentworth's hand tightened on the phone. "You mean—"

"Miss Nita van Sloan. She is now my—er—guest."

"Prove it!" Wentworth's knuckles were white on the phone.

"Easily. Naturally, knowing the kind of man you are, I expected that you would demand proof. I have here a phonograph record of a speech which I caused Miss van Sloan to make. I will now play it for you. Listen closely."

WENTWORTH WAS leaning over the desk with the phone at his ear. Stanton was watching him closely, guessing at the nature of the conversation. Kirkpatrick was no longer there. He had stepped out of the office, unnoticed.

Wentworth's lips were tight, his eyes bleak. He reached over the desk, and snatched up the tube of Kirkpatrick's Dictaphone machine, which was close alongside. He flipped over the recording key, then held the speaking tube of the Dictaphone close to

96

the mouthpiece of the telephone, just as the clear voice of Nita van Sloan came over the instrument. Stanton crowded closer, to hear:

"Dick, I am a prisoner of Professor Secundus. I have consented to make this recording because I realize now that it is useless to try to oppose him. Please believe me when I say that it is best to agree to all his terms. The Professor asks me to assure Mayor Stanton that Mary is unharmed. He tells me that you will be blind in twelve hours unless you get another dose of the serum. He will give it to you, if you meet his terms. Please agree, Dick, and remember always that I loved you."

Wentworth listened to that record with eyes closed, concentrating furiously. From the very first sentence he had caught the faint stressing of certain words in the set speech, which she had no doubt written down, and which Secundus had okayed. There was a queer gleam in his eyes when he opened them at the end of the record.

Stanton began to whisper excitedly, but he waved him to silence. Secundus was speaking once more.

"There is your proof, Wentworth. Do you need more?"

"No," he said.

"Then you believe that I have her prisoner?"

"Yes."

"Excellent. Then listen to my terms. You will withdraw the money—a hundred thousand dollars in small bills—and go with it to the broadcasting studio of WKL. There, you will make a speech at ten-thirty. WKL is a small station, and they have no sponsored program at that time. They will be glad to sell you fifteen minutes on the air for tomorrow morning. You will arrange for all that tonight."

"What sort of speech am I to make?"

"You will address the people of New York. You will state that Miss van Sloan is in the hands of Professor Secundus, and knowing it is hopeless to resist, you are paying off. Such a statement coming from you, will be of great assistance to me in breaking down the resistance of others."

"And if I do all this," Wentworth asked, "you will set Miss van Sloan free unharmed?"

"Yes."

Wentworth's voice dropped to a low pitch, but took on a sudden intensity. "Secundus, I think you are a liar!"

"Then you won't agree to my terms?"

"No."

"I am so sorry, Mr. Wentworth. It is too bad. Miss van Sloan and Miss Stanton will both pay for your stubbornness. You shall have until eight o'clock tomorrow morning to change your mind. But before that, I shall give the city a demonstration of my power that will utterly convince you."

"Wait!" Wentworth cried hoarsely. "What is this thing that you are going to do?"

"Hitherto," Secundus said softly, "I have contented myself with small-scale operations, believing that they would be sufficient to convince the authorities that they must meet my terms unconditionally. But I see that they are not yet convinced. So for tonight I have planned a little special event. It shall be an event which will cause more misery and destruction in a single hour than has been caused so far in the whole European War. After that, my dear Wentworth, there will be little question of the acquiescence of the authorities—"

"Look here!" Wentworth exclaimed "Suppose—" But Secundus was gone.

MAYOR STANTON was standing close to Wentworth. He had heard. "Good God, Wentworth," he croaked, "what is this event? What does that devil plan to do?"

Wentworth's face was a cold and frozen mask. "I have no idea."

The door opened, and Kirkpatrick came in. "Dick," he said in a low voice, "I was listening in. We've got to stop that man! We don't have to worry about Nita and Mary. If you comply with his terms, he'll free them—"

"No, Kirk," Wentworth said in a flat voice. "Secundus won't spare them. Nita told me so."

"Told you! What do you mean?"

Wentworth tapped the Dictaphone record.

Mayor Stanton and Kirkpatrick both looked blank. "How—how do you know?" Stanton demanded. "How did she tell you? I—I heard that record too. She advised you to yield—"

"That's what it sounded like," Wentworth said with a bitter smile. "But she told me all I need to know, in her last words. Shall I run it back for you on the Dictaphone, or shall I say them for you? Remember, she said: *'Remember always that I loved you!'* She didn't put it in the present tense. She put it in the past. She spoke as one already dead. Something she has observed convinces her that she is doomed. She deliberately said it that way, knowing I'd understand."

He pressed hot fingers against his temple. "But we mustn't think of Nita—or of Mary, now. We must think of this other thing—this event, which Secundus promises before midnight. If I'm any judge of the man's capacity for evil, many thousands of people will die or be blinded tonight, as a lesson to the city. If we could only get the analysis of the serum—perhaps we could manufacture enough antidote—"

Kirkpatrick snapped his fingers.

He reached over and picked up the inter-office phone, and asked for Nelson in the lab.

"What about it, Nelson?" he demanded.

Nelson's voice, dull and weary, came through the receiver. "I've finished the analysis. As near as I can determine, the fluid contained in the hypo is an ocular serum derived from some animal, probably a monkey, which has been previously inoculated with the glandular powder."

"Can you reproduce it?" Kirkpatrick demanded eagerly

Nelson's answer was a bitter laugh. "Yes. But it would take two years. The animals would have to be inoculated, then immunized. After that the serum could be extracted. By that time, every victim of Professor Secundus would be altogether beyond curing!"

"I see," said Kirkpatrick. "Thank you, Nelson."

He pronged the receiver, and faced Wentworth. "You heard, Dick. What are we going to do? *What are we going to do?*"

Wentworth turned his back on the Commissioner and went

to the window. For a long time he stood there, not moving. Then he turned and faced Kirkpatrick, looking him straight in the eyes.

"Kirk," he said, "let me have Ram Singh. And let me go my way tonight, without asking me any questions. Let me do what I must do tonight, and never make me explain."

Commissioner Kirkpatrick studied him for a full minute. "You—have an idea, Dick?"

Wentworth said nothing. He only waited for his answer.

Kirkpatrick took out a cigar and viciously bit the end off. "It—it has something to do with the Spider, hasn't it?"

Wentworth's face was expressionless. "You must ask me no questions, Kirk. I may hate myself forever for the thing I may have to do tonight. At least spare me the torture of talking about it."

The Commissioner glanced over toward Mayor Stanton, who nodded.

Kirkpatrick took the cigar out of his mouth. The end was in shreds.

"All right, Dick," he said in a strange voice. "For whatever you do tonight you shall never be asked an explanation—*if you succeed in averting the catastrophe!*"

"If I fail," Wentworth told him with a bitter smile, "I shall not worry about answering questions!"

He turned and walked out of the room in silence, with the eyes of the two men upon his straight, broad back.

CHAPTER 9
MESSAGE FROM NITA

R AM SINGH was pacing up and down like a caged lion in a room on the third floor, where he was being held pending the fixing of bail for him as a material witness.

Wentworth arranged for the Sikh to be released in his custody, promising to have him appear in court to testify at such time as Willie Hooke went on trial.

"Master," he said when they got down to the street floor. "I am a fool. I am worse than a fool. It was I who allowed Miss Nita to be kidnapped—"

"Not so, Ram Singh," said Wentworth. "You should know better than anyone that these things are written, and that they must happen. You are not to blame."

He took the Sikh's arm. "Tonight, old friend, we shall make the most desperate gamble of our lives—you and I!"

"Inshallah!" exclaimed Ram Singh, his eyes glittering. "And shall there be some good fighting, Master? Shall we have a chance to strike a blow at these pigs?"

Wentworth shrugged. "I hope so."

The Sikh smiled. "Let us begin, Master!"

Wentworth pressed his arm, and led the way out into the street. Dick was carrying a cylindrical object, wrapped in thick folds of newspaper. It was the Dictaphone record upon which he had taken down the speech recorded by Nita, and which Professor had played into the telephone for him. He slipped the record into his pocket.

102

In the street he looked up and down sharply, then followed the Sikh to the Daimler, which was parked in front of the building.

"I believe someone will follow us, Ram Singh," he said, as they pulled away from the curb. "There is no doubt that Secundus has one or more men watching police headquarters, for he knew that I was here, almost before I entered the building."

"*Wah!*" said Ram Singh. "If the pigs follow us, it will be a chance to break some heads—"

"No," said Wentworth. "Not yet. For the present we shall seem not to notice them. Drive to the Fifth Avenue apartment."

Richard Wentworth's name was listed in the telephone directory as residing in the Park Arms on Fifth Avenue, facing Central Park. That was his official residence. Few people knew about the other retreats he maintained in the city. It was from the Park Arms address, though, that he conducted all of his business, and directed his charitable activities. If he were being followed, it would seem to his trailers the most natural place for him to go now.

They had gone only a few blocks when they became aware of the tan sedan which was keeping pace with them about a block behind.

"It is the same one," Ram Singh said fiercely, "that followed Miss Nita and myself when we left her apartment!"

"Good!" said Wentworth. His eyes were frosty. "I hope it contains the same men!"

When they arrived at the Park Arms, they left the Daimler at the front door and hurried up in the elevator to the penthouse which Wentworth occupied on the roof of the building.

ONCE INSIDE, Wentworth proceeded directly into his study, while Ram Singh went out the back way, taking the service elevator down to the rear of the building. He was going to scout around to spy out the location of those who had followed them. He had his master's orders merely to check on how many had been left to watch the building. Like a good general, Wentworth liked to know the exact dispositions made by the enemy, so that he would not have to move blindly when the time came to act.

He himself took the Dictaphone record from his pocket, and fitted it into his Dictaphone machine. Then he took paper and pencil, and started the record playing.

He played it over three times, listening tautly to every inflection of Nita's voice, running it through very slowly, and copying down the words. He underlined those words which she had stressed faintly. He had noticed that slight accentuation, and he was sure it meant something.

At last, he had the whole speech copied and properly underlined. He shut off the Dictaphone, and studied the paper. It looked something like this:

> Dick, I am a prisoner *of* Professor *Secundus*. I have consented to make this recording *because I realize*....

He frowned at the written words. Those that were underlined did not seem to have any connection with each other. If Nita had been trying to convey a message, she could not have had much time, between writing it down and broadcasting it, in which to work out a complicated code. It would have to be simple, and it could not be one of those codes which they had often used together, based on association with the Bible or Shakespeare, for he was sure that she did not have access to any books where she was being held.

He took another sheet of paper and made a list of the stressed words: *a, of, Secundus, because, I, realize, is, to, to, say, that, it, to, his, the, that, Mary, is, that, will, blind, dose, of, the, it, you, you, remember, always, that.*

He studied those words, rearranged them, juggling them, seeking possible equivalents. The repetition of words bothered him, as well as the use of the proper nouns *Mary* and *Secundus.* A code using proper nouns would of necessity have to be an arbitrary one, with equivalents arranged beforehand.

He tried discarding the accented words, and using the others. While he was working on these, Ram Singh returned and reported.

"There are five of the pigs, Master. A man with the face of an angel is their leader. He has blue eyes, and he looks as if he were the most innocent man in the world. He and another are watching the front of the building. Two are in the rear, and one has gone into the lobby to question the doorman. The two in the rear have gone down into the basement, and they are working with the telephone wires."

"That's good, Ram Singh," Wentworth said absently. He was concentrating all his faculties on the cipher, and Ram Singh watched him understandingly, knowing that there was no way in which he could help, except by being silent. After a long time, he heaved a sigh of deep disappointment when Dick threw down the pencil, and got up from the desk.

"It's no use," Wentworth said bitterly. "Miss Nita is trying to tell me something in that message—and I can't get it!"

Ram Singh suddenly gripped his arm. "Ps-st, Master. They come!" The Sikh's ears were like those of a cat. He had heard a noise which Wentworth had not caught.

"They come through the rear service entrance, which I left open, Master. There are three—no, four—"

Wentworth's lips were grim and tight.

"Everything is ready, Ram Singh?"

"Yes, Master."

WENTWORTH FLIPPED open the front of a box on his desk. It was equipped with two small switches, and four tiny bulbs. The extreme left hand bulb was flashing red, intermittently.

"That shows they are in the Conservatory," Wentworth murmured. In a moment the next light flashed on, and the first went off.

"In the music room," Ram Singh whispered. They watched while the third bulb flashed. "Now they are in the corridor!" The eyes of both men were glued to the box. Wentworth put out a hand and gripped one of the switches. They waited until the third light went out, and the fourth flashed on.

"They are in the gun room, Master!"

"Now!" said Wentworth, and pulled the switch. At once there was a screeching sound, followed by a loud slam. Then, utter silence. Ram Singh breathed a deep sigh. "The sliding door has closed. They are locked in, Master!"

Wentworth nodded. He pushed away the Dictaphone and the scrawled papers, and rose to his feet. Slowly he walked across the room, followed by the Sikh. He went out into the hall, and entered a small room off the hall.

The walls of this room were lined with what appeared to be bookcases. But they did not contain books. The shelves were loaded with tubes and vials of all kinds, neatly labeled in code. At one end of the room there was a platform, with a large picture of Pasteur above it.

Wentworth went to one of the cases and unlocked it. He took out a vial labeled, *"M-23."* Donning a pair of rubber gloves, he took from another case a large, bellows-like affair which resembled a syringe, except that the muzzle was shaped like the muzzle of an old-style blunderbuss. He unscrewed the cap of the vial, and swiftly applied the open mouth to an opening in the bellows. Then he drew the contents of the vial into the bellows.

He raised his head and saw Ram Singh looking at him with glittering eyes. The Sikh nodded. "Have no remorse, Master. It is no more than these pigs deserve."

Wentworth did not answer. He stepped up on the platform, and removed the picture of Pasteur. Behind it there was a panel in the wall. He pressed a button, and the panel slid open.

There was another picture on the other side of the wall, facing into the next room. It covered the opening revealed by the sliding panel. That other room was the Gun Room, where the four invaders had been trapped by the sliding door. The upper walls of the Gun Room were covered by pictures depicting hunting scenes, and the four men in there could not tell that someone was watching them. But Wentworth could see them, for there were ingenious spy-holes in the picture, which could not be noticed from the floor of the Gun Room.

He peered through these holes, and saw the four gunmen moving tensely around the room, trying all the doors and windows. He smiled tightly. There was not a chance of their getting out. The doors were lined with sheet steel, and the windows were covered entirely with the same material. The only light in the room came from an indirect system high in the ceiling.

Ram Singh climbed up beside Wentworth, and they both watched those four men, noting how their anxiety increased with each passing moment as they discovered that there was no visible mode of egress from the room.

At last, Wentworth sighed. He raised his voice.

"Men," he said, "you are trapped."

At the sound of his words, the thugs jumped as if they had been shot. They all had guns in their hands, and they raised the weapons, seeking a target. But the acoustics of the room were such that it was impossible to tell the direction from which the voice had come. They looked nervously at each other, then turned and stared at the walls. They were frightened. They weren't used to being on the receiving end of this sort of thing. WENTWORTH WAITED a while, then he spoke again. "You have been sent here to kill me or capture me. But the tables are turned. You are in my hands. I want information. Who is your master? Who is Professor Secundus?"

One of the other men tugged at an unkempt shock of black hair, snarled, "Go to hell, mister. You better let us outta here fast, or you can figure what'll happen to your pretty girlfriend." He leered up into space, not knowing in which direction to address himself. "The Professor says we don't have to worry. To come and take you and bring you back. And he says you won't offer any resistance, because you'll be thinking of what might happen to that baby of yours."

One of the other men tugged at the big fellow's sleeve. "Take it easy, Blackie. You don't have to get him sore."

"Nuts!" snarled Blackie. "He knows the Professor's got his girl."

"Yes, Blackie," Wentworth said ominously, "I know it. And I'm asking you to talk—quickly. Before I do something I shall be sorry for to the end of time."

"Go ahead," Blackie barked. "Go ahead. Only remember, your girl pays for it!"

Wentworth sighed, and looked down at the bellows in his hands. He glanced at Ram Singh, who whispered, "Do not hesitate, Master. This is war. In war with beasts there can be no mercy."

Wentworth's mouth was set and hard. "Men," he called out, "I have here a quantity of mustard gas. You all know what mustard gas will do to you. If one of you does not talk within three minutes, I shall release the gas into the room. Begin now. I shall not warn you again. At the end of three minutes, the gas will come!"

He stopped talking, and nodded grimly to Ram Singh, who turned and fixed his eyes on the electric clock on the other wall.

For the first minute there was utter silence in the other room. The four men stood looking at each other, each thinking his own thoughts. Then they began to fidget. They were all stealing glances at their wrist watches, furtively glancing in all directions.

"One minute gone, Master," Ram Singh said.

Wentworth stood immovable, holding the bellows ready.

One of the men down in the Gun Room snapped his fingers nervously. "Gawd, Blackie, I think he'll do it! Gawd! Mustard gas! It burns your insides out!"

"Shut up, Lister!" Blackie growled. "He won't do it."

Lister subsided, but he kept looking around, cringing as if to avoid the invisible mustard gas which he would not be able to see when it came.

"Two minutes, Master," Ram Singh said in a steady voice.

Wentworth's grip tightened on the bellows. His face was white.

Down below, Lister looked at his wrist watch. "Gawd!" he shrieked. "I can't stand it. I can't—"

Blackie struck him a backhanded blow in the face that sent him sprawling to the floor. "Shut up! Wait'll you see. Nothing will happen!"

"Three minutes, Master!" Ram Singh said.

Wentworth took a deep breath. He started to raise the bellows, and then jerked them down. "I can't—"

"Master!" Ram Singh's big hard fingers dug into his shoulder. "You are a man, and you have given your word that you will do it. You must. It is the lives of thousands—and the life of Mistress Nita—against four swine!"

Blackie was saying triumphantly, "See! Didn't I tell you? He dassen't try it—"

Grimly, Wentworth placed the mouth of the bellows at one of the holes, and shot the gas into the room.

He sent in only one shot, then stopped.

The gas was colorless, but not entirely invisible, for it formed a whitish cloud that drifted down toward the floor of the Gun Room, and began to thin out as it mingled with the air.

Lister was the first to see the white cloud. He screamed, and pointed.

"There it is! Gawd, there it is!"

BLACKIE AND the others followed his pointing finger, and their eyes widened. They all began to back away. But it did them no good. One of them began to cough, and then the others. Deep, wracking coughs tore at their bodies. But that only lasted a short while, for the dose of gas had been very small.

Wentworth called out, "That was the first shot. Here comes more. I shall feed it to you until you all die in agony!"

"No, no!" Lister shrieked. "You couldn't do that to us. It—it ain't human!"

"No," Wentworth told him. "It isn't human. But *I'm* not human tonight. I'll do *anything* to save the people who are to die tonight. *Anything*. Do you understand? Here comes the second dose. Whoever wants to be spared, had better talk quickly."

He started to press the bellows, and Lister screamed, "Wait! I'll talk!"

The others began to babble, each vying with the other.

Wentworth breathed a deep sigh of relief. He wiped perspiration from his forehead.

"Ram Singh," he whispered, "I couldn't have gone through with it!"

The Sikh smiled, showing his white teeth. "I would have done it for you, Master!"

Wentworth addressed the men below. "I want to know the name of your master. *Who is Professor Secundus?*"

The four men down there looked blankly at each other. Lister raised terrified eyes to the wall.

"God help us all, mister, we don't know that. We take orders over the phone, but we never saw Professor Secundus!"

"You lie," said Wentworth.

"No, no! I swear it!"

The others raised their voices in chorus, supporting Lister's statement.

"Where are your headquarters then?" Wentworth demanded.

Blackie answered that one. "We don't know. We are picked up by an ambulance, and we don't see a thing till we're inside."

"I see," Wentworth said softly.

"Then you'll not use the mustard gas?" Lister demanded eagerly.

"Yes," Wentworth said sternly. "I shall use it. I think you're all lying. You haven't told me what I want to know!"

"Wait!" Lister shrieked. "Wait!"

"Well?"

Lister licked his lips. "I—I swear I don't know who Professor Secundus is. But—but I can tell you something important—about tonight!"

Wentworth became tense.

"Well?"

"We—" Lister paused, then looked at Blackie and the others, who nodded, urging him to go ahead—"We have a job to do tonight. At midnight. If—if we told you where the job is—would you—would you let us go?"

"I'll make no bargains till I hear what you have to say," Wentworth told him.

"All right, we'll tell you. It—it's at the Gaynor Auditorium. We're to report there at midnight—and bring you."

"The Gaynor Auditorium!" Wentworth gasped. "That's where they're holding the midnight Benefit Performance for the relief of the blinded victims of Professor Secundus!"

"That's right," Lister said eagerly. "All the stars of stage and screen are going to perform, and they're going to raise money."

"Three thousand people!" Wentworth whispered to Ram Singh. "That's where Secundus intends to strike! He's going to kill or blind all those three thousand people—while they're trying to raise funds to help other victims whom he has already blinded!"

Lister was saying, "Is that what you wanted to know? Will you let us go now?"

"I'll not let you go," Wentworth told him, "until after I've verified your story. If we succeed in saving those people, you four

113

men may go free, and I will see that you are permitted to leave the country. Otherwise, you will hear from me again."

"Wait," Blackie called out. "There's one thing more you gotta know—as long as our freedom depends on it. My orders were to take the boys up there, and to watch the streets. If we notice any large body of police, we're to give a signal. That signal will start things moving. And there will be other watchers in the street. So if you want to stop this, don't bring in the police!"

"I see," said Wentworth. "All right, men. You will be taken care of as soon as we return. There's not much time—twenty minutes before midnight."

He climbed down from the platform. "Come, Ram Singh!"

IT WAS only eleven minutes later that a dark, gliding shadow insinuated itself into a narrow alley behind the great Gaynor Auditorium. At the front, the huge building, with a seating capacity of three thousand, was brilliantly illuminated, with a great electric sign announcing the Benefit Performance with an admission charge of ten dollars. All the wealthy and philanthropic families of the city were represented here tonight, and the boxes within were a blaze of brilliance, reflecting untold fortunes in jewels and diamonds.

But out in back here, there was only darkness, and a few patrolmen posted as routine duty, and the gliding shadow of a man.

This man moved swiftly yet purposefully. He found a side entrance to the building, and tried the door. It was locked, but in a matter of moments he had it open, and was inside.

The beautiful voice of a famous coloratura soprano came

114

wafting back from the immense hall at the front of the building, immediately followed by thunderous applause. The Benefit was in full swing. At midnight exactly, the Mayor was scheduled to make his appearance with a plea for contributions. Ten minutes to go now. Ten minutes more, and the vicious army of Professor Secundus would strike.

The gliding shadow passed down a flight of stairs, and flitted under a dim electric bulb. It was revealed as the figure of a man in a great black cape, and with a slouch hat pulled low over his face. To any member of the underworld who might have glimpsed him at the moment, his appearance and name were familiar—and terrible.

The Spider was walking again tonight.

The Spider hurried soundlessly down into the sub-basement, and tried a door marked, "Air-conditioning." It was unlocked. Before opening it he reached up and turned out the bulb which lit the hallway. Then he pushed the door open.

The huge room which was revealed, contained the great blowers which sent fresh air into the auditorium. The machinery was whirring as usual. But the scene which met the Spider's eyes was far from normal.

Three men in mechanics' overalls were lying sprawled upon the floor, in pools of blood, where they had been struck down. And in their places were a motley crew of thugs, manning the switches and blowers. Two of the thugs were standing at the main blower, and watching the clock. One of them had his hand on the intake valve, ready to open it. The other was holding a can with a spout on it.

There were three other thugs in the room, standing guard with drawn guns. It was not difficult to guess the purpose of these men. At the stroke of midnight they would pour the blinding powder into the intake valve, and the blowers would carry it up and spray it into the great auditorium. Three thousand people would be struck blind.

One of the guards was saying, "Boy, it'll be a cinch for the boys upstairs to clean out that crowd. Imagine them, all milling around blind, and the guys grabbing all that dough they brought for contributions—"

He broke off sharply as another guard cried, "Look out! The Spider!"

The man raised his gun and fired at the sinister shadow which had slipped into the room. The gun blasted deafeningly in the stone-vaulted basement. But the man should have been a fraction of a second quicker. For another gun in the hand of the Spider spat flame a split-instant sooner. The man went flailing backward, a black hole in his forehead.

The other two guards swung their guns toward the Spider, while the two at the blower dropped their can of poisonous powder and snatched for their weapons.

The Spider's black cape swirled ominously about his figure. He laughed, deep down in his chest. There was a gun in each hand now, and he held them low, at his hips, firing coldly and methodically.

Each shot registered a hit. Thunder rolled back from the walls of the basement—thunder which would not be heard upstairs due to the soundproofing of the building, and due also to the fact that the air-conditioning blowers were still closed. So that those who were viewing the entertainment above had no means of knowing that men were dying here below, under the blazing guns of one who never expected to receive their thanks.

THOSE GUNMEN fired frantically and wildly, but even as they pulled triggers they knew that they were doomed. Time and again they had heard strange tales of the sinister Spider, whose two guns wreaked terrible vengeance against the vicious killers of the underworld. Time and again they had heard of the uncanny speed and accuracy of the cloaked Nemesis of crime, and they had laughed nervously and boasted that they were not afraid, for no man could shoot so well, nor was any man proof against their own bullets.

But tonight they had a chance to learn differently. They learned their lesson, but it profited them not one bit, for they died in the learning.

When the gun fire died down and the cordite fumes cleared away, the Spider raised the muzzles of his two smoking guns and let his glittering eyes rest for a second upon the dead. Then he ran forward swiftly and knelt at the side of each gunman, doing something with swift and sure fingers. When he was finished he hurried out of the room, reloading as he went.

But back in that basement there were five dead men, each with a peculiar mark upon his forehead—the crimson seal of the Spider. When they were found, all men would know that the Spider had been here and exacted retribution. Another chapter would be added to the never-ending legend of the Spider!— Master of Men.

But at this moment the black-cloaked figure was not thinking of that. He was racing up the stairs, glancing at his wrist watch.

Two minutes of twelve. At midnight sharp, if he had understood aright from the remark of one of the gunmen down there, the armed thugs of Professor Secundus would erupt upon the startled audience of the hall, for the purpose of looting them. They would expect to find that audience rendered helpless and blind, and they would be surprised. But they would still be armed, whereas the men and women present at the Benefit would have no weapons. There would be slaughter. It must be stopped.

The Spider reached the main floor as the hands of the clock pointed to forty-five seconds before midnight. He came out into the hall through the fire-door, and found himself in a passageway behind the stage. From where he stood he could see actors and stagehands, all with their eyes upon the platform, where Mayor Stanton was arising to begin his address. None of them noticed the shadowy figure who moved toward the wings.

But one man who was watching for him, did not fail to see him. That was Ram Singh. The Sikh, armed with an automatic rifle of latest make, was waiting at the end of the passageway, in accordance with instructions Wentworth had previously given him. "Master!" he exclaimed. "All went well below?"

The Spider nodded. "Yes. We must move quickly though, to stop needless slaughter up here. Take the front entrance, Ram Singh. If you see any of these thugs, shoot to kill. If the lobby is empty, come to the front entrance of the hall and back up any play I make!" The Sikh, a born fighting man, waited not even to repeat the orders. He darted away.

The Spider sprang forward and reached the wings. He thrust aside a couple of stagehands, and stepped toward the stage, though he was still hidden from the audience by the wing curtain.

Mayor Stanton was saying, "My friends, we are all assembled here on an errand of mercy…" He stopped as a commotion sounded at the rear of the orchestra. A close-knit, compact group of thugs suddenly appeared, armed with submachine guns. Their leader, a short man with a close-cropped bullet head, raised his voice.

"Everybody keep your seats. You're being blinded. But if you move, we'll kill you, and that'll be worse. Empty your pockets as my men go down the aisle. Anybody who holds out will get a slug in the belly!"

It was at that moment which the Spider chose to make his appearance. He brushed aside the curtain and stepped out on to the stage. Mayor Stanton saw him first, and gasped. Then his gasp was echoed by the startled audience, which was already in a state of panic. The Spider had a gun in each hand.

"You are in no danger of being blinded," he shouted to the audience: "I have taken care of that. The only danger is from this handful of armed rats!"

The leader of the thugs jerked around to look at the stage, and screamed. "The Spider! Get him!" Machine-guns were jerked to shoulders, and vicious slitted eyes were applied to sights. But already the two guns of the Spider were blazing from the stage.

The panic of the audience had no time to gain momentum, so swiftly did the action unfold. They were rooted to the seats by the thunderous detonations of the Spider's two heavy forty-fives, augmented as the sound was by the acoustic properties of the hall.

HIS GUNS blasted twin streams of death into the mob of gangsters, and in a moment a second sound was added—the high, whining drone of high-caliber bullets spitting from Ram Singh's automatic rifle at the back of the hall.

The gangsters were mowed down by that crossfire with merciless accuracy. Those who remained standing threw down their guns and raised their hands in the air, screaming frantically for mercy.

The Spider stopped shooting, and so did Ram Singh.

"Ladies and gentlemen," the Spider said, wrapping his cloak about him and bowing courteously, "I leave these thugs to your tender mercies."

And as quickly as he had appeared upon the stage, he disappeared.

For a moment the audience sat in stunned silence, realizing with difficulty what their peril had been, and how they had been saved. Then, one of the thugs turned and started to run for the exit.

Immediately, a low growl of rage arose from some of the men in the audience. They leaped to their feet and fell on the fleeing gunmen. All the hate and all the despair which had filled their breasts for the past week as the outrages of Professor Secundus were repeated and repeated, now was vented upon these killers of Secundus'. Their screams filled the air, as they were buried under a frenzied mass of men, eager to avenge loved ones.

Outside, in the night, two men stood and listened. Ram Singh's black eyes glittered in the darkness.

"It is just, Master, that they should be punished by the people they have wronged. It is a law of life."

Wentworth was grave. "They deserved it, but—poor devils— I'm sorry for them!"

He put a hand on Ram Singh's shoulder.

"Come, old friend. We have something more to do. When Secundus learns of this, he will vent *his* rage upon Nita and Mary. We must wrack our brains for a way to find them!"

Their car was a block away. As Ram Singh tooled it from the curb, they heard the screech of police sirens on the way to the Gaynor Auditorium. But neither of them looked back. They were looking forward—with hope and dread—wondering whether they would be able to save another whom they loved, as they had been able to save the terrified patrons of the Benefit.

Back in the apartment, Wentworth strode up and down in his study, pressing his fists against his throbbing temples as he tried vainly to make sense of the Dictaphone message which Nita had spoken over the phone. He played it over and over again, and wrote it down in a dozen different ways. He was no more successful than he had been before.

Twice he was interrupted by telephone calls from Commissioner Kirkpatrick, who told him what had happened at the Gaynor Auditorium, but faithfully refrained from asking any questions.

Ram Singh went to the Gun Room and fed emetics to the four imprisoned thugs, and made arrangements for them to leave the country, as Wentworth had promised them. When the Sikh returned, he brought coffee for his master, which Wentworth gulped, hot and black. Wentworth glared at the papers upon which he had scrawled a dozen different versions of Nita's message. He rapped a fist into the palm of his hand.

"It's no use, Ram Singh. It's there—I'm sure. Nita meant to convey a message. But I can't get it!"

RAM SINGH began to drum nervously on the window sill. "*Wah*, Master. Do not rack your brains. Let us go down and bring up one of those pigs. With my knife I will cut him to pieces bit by bit, until he talks."

Wentworth shook his head. "Those men don't know anything. Secundus wouldn't trust any one man with enough information to betray him."

"But we can try, Master," the Sikh said hopefully.

Once more he began to drum with his fingertips on the windowsill, watching Wentworth pace up and down, from one end of the room to the other, in desperate concentration.

He kept on drumming, drumming… Suddenly, Wentworth jerked his head up, and snapped his fingers. "I've got it, Ram Singh!" He snatched up the pencil, and began to make dots under unstressed words, dashes under the accented ones.

"It's Morse Code, Ram Singh; Here, look: 'Dick, I am'—that's three dots. Then she accents *a*—that's a dash. Three dots and a dash make 'V' in Morse. Let's see how it works out!"

Ram Singh watched his flying pencil eagerly, as he marked

the dots and dashes under the words of the entire message. In a few moments he had it completed, and the two of them stared down at it. Wentworth's eyes were narrow and thoughtful. The message as decoded, looked something like this:

V END IS O NVEND IS ON V END

"Vendisson!" exclaimed Wentworth. "The message repeats the name—*Vendisson!*"

"*Inshallah!*" murmured Ram Singh. "Is that not the great physician of the eyes and the ears who even now tries to work to cure those unfortunates who have been blinded?"

"Yes, Ram Singh."

"*Missy Sahib* wishes then, that you should consult this great physician?"

"I doubt it. I think she's trying to tell us that Vendisson is— Professor Secundus!"

"By Allah, Master, if that is the case, then this Doctor Vendisson is the most evil of men in all the world. For he takes back into his power all those poor unfortunates who think that he will try to cure them. It is a terrible thing to think about, Master. If it is true, then he is one whose neck I should like to take lovingly into these two hands of mine!"

Wentworth's own hands were clenched on the desk. "And yet, what is more logical? Vendisson, eh! I've never met him. But he would be in a wonderful position to work a thing like this!"

"Then call Commissioner Kirkpatrick, Master. Tell him of this, that he may send men to raid the hospital of this devil-doctor—"

He stopped, seeing Wentworth shaking his head. "I'm afraid that's no good, Ram Singh. Vendisson would surely not lay himself open to having anything easily discovered in the hospital. If he is Professor Secundus, you can be sure that he has taken precautions, so that nothing will be found there in case of a raid. I'm sure that the best way to bring about the quick death of Nita and Mary Stanton would be to raid the place!"

The Sikh looked helpless. He was used to direct action. When he was told what to do, he did it in the quickest and most direct method, regardless of what danger stood in the way. But this was different.

Wentworth snatched up the phone, and dialed Police Headquarters.

"Remember, Master," Ram Singh whispered, "that there are those below who listen in!"

WENTWORTH NODDED; his lips tight; he got his call put through. "Say, Kirk," he drawled, "I've been thinking since I left you, you know." *Now he must be careful. He must not say too much, or too little!* "What about that young fellow that was blinded this evening—that escaped convict. What's his name?"

"Blair," said Kirkpatrick. "Jack Blair What about him, Dick?"

"I was wondering if we shouldn't run over and talk to him—"

"No go, Dick. He's over at Doctor Vendisson's Hospital, and the doctor reports that he's still in a delirious condition. It was necessary to give him a strong opiate. It's a waste of time going to see Blair."

"Nevertheless," Wentworth said smoothly, "I should like to look at him. How about meeting me, and we can run over there?"

124

"Well, I hate to take the time, Dick. I expect to be down here all night. There's so much to do. Better skip it—"

Wentworth felt like shouting, *Damn you, Kirk, don't spoil the play. Don't fall down on me now. Don't you see, we've got to have a reason for going there?*

Instead, he said, "Well, all right, Kirk, if you haven't the time. Maybe I'll run over there myself. I'd like to find out if there's a chance for him. I know Jack Blair's family, and I owe it to them to visit the kid."

"With so much on your mind," Kirkpatrick grunted, "you can think of what you owe to a convict's family! You're a queer bird, Dick. What would Nita say if she knew that you were paying social calls at a time like this?"

Wentworth wanted to blurt, *God, Kirk, you can be exasperating!* But what he did say was, "I'm sure Nita would want me to go, Kirk. If you can't get away, I'll go alone. And I wish you could spare the time. I'd like to have you stop in with me at Station WKL, and lend official support to my request for time tomorrow morning. I want to be sure they don't turn me down."

At last he had the Commissioner's interest. "Then you'll do it? You'll make the broadcast? You've decided to pay Secundus?"

"Well, not quite. But I'd like to have the time arranged for, in case I decide to do it. After all, there's so much at stake—"

"Dick," Kirkpatrick interrupted, "Mayor Stanton will be glad to hear that."

Yes, thought Wentworth. *And there's somebody else who's no doubt glad to hear it!*

Kirkpatrick hurried on, "I'll tell Stanton there's a good chance you'll do it. He's on the verge of a nervous breakdown, thinking of what will happen to Mary if you refuse. And look, Dick, I'll run up there, and go with you. If you think there's a chance of you making the broadcast, I'd like to talk it over with you. God knows, I—of all people—shouldn't be urging you to surrender to this fiend, but I can't stand to think of Nita and Mary being blinded. It's too much of a price to pay. I'll be right over!"

Wentworth hung up, feeling like a wet rag. He had put it over, he thought, without arousing the suspicions of those who were tapping his wire. They would no doubt report at once to Professor Secundus that Kirkpatrick and Wentworth were going to the hospital. If Vendisson was Secundus, then the doctor would have ample time to cover up, and that was what Wentworth wanted. He didn't want him to be scared by a sudden police visit, or even by a visit from himself, into making away with Nita van Sloan and Mary Stanton.

"All right, Ram Singh," he said. "We're starting. And from this minute on, watch your step!"

"I will watch, Master," the Sikh said, showing his teeth. "And I will wait—for the time when I may take the neck of Professor Secundus in these two hands, and break it!

CHAPTER 10
THE SPIDER BROADCASTS

THE VENDISSON EYE AND EAR HOSPI-TAL was a beautiful product of the most advanced architectural skill of the year 1940. It has been financed by leading citizens of the community. Doctor Vendisson, however, retained complete control of all administrative activities, and was responsible to no one.

The graceful building was eleven floors high, with corner windows, great expanses of glass, and setbacks at every other floor. The ground had been donated by the Empire Crematory, which occupied the low building adjoining.

It is the tragedy of mankind that human nature is so constituted as to cause men to thirst for power rather than to fulfill the manifest destiny for which his peculiar abilities fit him. Thus, an Austrian house-painter longs to rule the world with an iron fist, a Georgian peasant dreams of building himself an empire stretching from the Arctic to the Indian Ocean; and a brilliant doctor yearns to rule America.

As Ram Singh tooled the Daimler in along the circular driveway approaching the hospital's main entrance, Wentworth, sitting in the rear with Kirkpatrick, thought that if Nita's message were true, and Vendisson were really Professor Secundus, then here was a dreadful example of the lengths to which a man will go in the effort to achieve power.

He had told Kirkpatrick very little of what he had discovered. In the first place, he feared Kirkpatrick's immediate disbelief of any statement incriminating Doctor Vendisson—unless it were accompanied by absolute proof. And of proof he had not one iota. In the second place, though he had great respect for the Commissioner's ability as a law-enforcer, he feared that Kirkpatrick's acting ability would not be equal to concealing the real purpose of the visit.

They had stopped in at WKL on the way over, and arranged for fifteen minutes of time the following morning. And now they were here at the hospital.

Kirkpatrick muttered, "This looks to me like a fool's errand, Dick. There are so many other things to do tonight. We could just as easily have called Vendisson and asked him if Blair was in shape to talk."

"Perhaps you're right, Kirk," Wentworth said. "But as long as we're here, we might as well go in. Then I can at least tell Jack's family that I went to see him."

As they were mounting the steps to the front entrance, Wentworth turned and nodded to Ram Singh who was at the wheel of the Daimler, and the Sikh showed his teeth in a wide grin and drove away.

Kirkpatrick frowned. "Say, where's Ram Singh going? Why doesn't he wait for us? We're not staying long—"

"Of course not, Kirk. Ram Singh will be here when we're ready to leave."

WENTWORTH TOLD him that absently, for he was watching the tan sedan which had followed them from his apartment to the broadcasting station, and then here. He now saw that the sedan was parked directly opposite the hospital. They were not following the Daimler any longer, but were remaining here to watch Wentworth.

They were greeted by a courteous male attendant at the desk, and Wentworth asked if they could see Jack Blair. The man did not seem too surprised that they should be calling on a patient at this hour of the night—it was after midnight—and told them to have a seat.

It was the first time Wentworth had been here, and he inspected everything with keen, cool, analyzing eyes. Inside, he was far from cool. Time was slipping away, inexorably. There were not so many hours to go before morning—morning, when his own sight would go, when he must capitulate to Professor Secundus and help to turn the whole city over to him to ravage and terrorize at will. Morning—when, he was sure, Nita would either be blinded or killed, regardless of whether he capitulated or not.

He started abruptly as he realized that Kirkpatrick was talking to him, exhibiting a small vial which he had taken from his vest pocket.

"... so I got the rest of the serum that Nelson didn't need to use for analysis, and brought it along. I'll give it to Doctor Vendisson. Maybe *he* can figure out a way how to manufacture it in a hurry—"

"I'd rather you didn't, Kirk," Wentworth said quickly.

"Why not?" Kirkpatrick asked, frowning. "Even if Vendisson can't duplicate it, he may be able to use what's left to save the eyesight of some poor devil of a patient—"

"I still prefer that you do not give it to Vendisson," Wentworth insisted. "I have something else in mind for it—"

"Nonsense, Dick. Vendisson is the one man in the city who can make the best use of it."

"Please don't forget that that serum is my property, Kirk. I'll ask you to give it back—"

Kirkpatrick shook his head stubbornly. "Not a chance, Dick. This serum is now public property."

Wentworth sighed. "There's something I've got to tell you, Kirk. I had hoped to prove it to you in the course of our visit here, but you force my hand."

Kirkpatrick frowned. "What is it, Dick?"

Wentworth said slowly, "Doctor Vendisson is Professor Secundus!"

FOR A moment Kirkpatrick stared at him speechless. Then he exploded. "Dick! You've gone mad!"

"No, Kirk. I'm afraid I'm utterly sane. There was a code message in that speech which Nita recorded. Want to see it?"

He took from his pocket the paper upon which he had written down the transcription of Nita's speech. He had the dots and dashes marked out for it, and the corresponding letters.

"See," he explained to the Commissioner, "she couldn't get over a long message, so she had to content herself with just giving a name—*Vendisson!*"

Kirkpatrick took the paper, looked from it to Wentworth. There was suspicion in his eyes.

"How do you know these words are dots, and the others dashes? How do—"

"Didn't you hear Nita?" Wentworth demanded. "She stressed certain words—"

"I'm sorry, Dick, but this is too far-fetched to be credible. Certainly I heard her talk. And I didn't notice that she stressed *any* words. I think you're nervous and overwrought by this whole business, so that you've come to the point where you are imagining fantastic things. Why it's preposterous to suspect Vendisson. I'll have nothing to do with it!"

A step sounded in the corridor, and Doctor Vendisson himself entered the room. He looked tired, but crisply efficient. He was wearing a white surgeon's coat over his vest, and his long, flexible fingers which were so skillful with a scalpel were busy adjusting the knot of his necktie. He was followed by a male nurse, who held a number of charts, but who remained outside in the corridor.

"Ah, good evening, Commissioner," said Doctor Vendisson. "I was told you were calling here, so I immediately came down." His glance, shifting from Kirkpatrick, came to rest for a fleeting instant upon Richard Wentworth.

Wentworth watched him tensely, studying his eyes. But there was no flicker of recognition in Vendisson's eyes. He merely looked at Wentworth half expectantly, as if awaiting an introduction. Either the man had never seen Wentworth before, or he was a supreme master of self-control, or he had had advance warning of the fact that Richard Wentworth was coming here with the Commissioner.

Kirkpatrick's face was still flushed from his altercation with Dick, but he introduced them.

Vendisson extended his hand cordially, smiling at Dick.

"I have heard a good deal about you, Mr. Wentworth. People speak highly of your ability as an amateur criminologist. Let us hope that you will be able to aid the police in quickly bringing this terrible Professor Secundus to book."

"Look here, Doctor," Kirkpatrick blurted. "We may as well

have this out, right here and now. Wentworth here, has a certain suspicion. He suspects that *you* are Professor Secundus, and that *you* are holding Nita van Sloan and Mary Stanton prisoners. I have too much respect for you to allow such a suspicion to remain in anyone's mind. Wentworth thinks that those girls are prisoners in this hospital. Suppose you let us go through the place, and convince him."

VENDISSON SEEMED to be both hurt and amazed by the blunt statement. But he did not allow himself to give way to anger or indignation. He turned slowly to Wentworth, looking at him without hostility.

"Please don't think that I am angry at this suspicion of yours, Mr. Wentworth. I realize that everybody's nerves are jittery these days. You are welcome to go through the entire hospital. Of course, you must realize how difficult it would be to conceal anybody held here against her will, in a large institution such as this. But if it will satisfy you, why go ahead."

Wentworth's blood was racing. He had difficulty in restraining himself from turning around and smashing his friend, Kirkpatrick, full in the face. Kirkpatrick had let the fat into the fire for fair. Now Vendisson would be thoroughly on guard. And of course, he had taken precautions against a possible search of the hospital.

Wentworth said, "No, I don't want to search this place. I didn't say that Nita and Mary were being held *here*. But I did say that *you* are Professor Secundus."

"But, my dear man," Vendisson protested, frowning, "surely you must have some grounds to back up such a statement.

132

Perhaps if you will tell me your reason, I may be able to set you right."

"No," said Wentworth. "I can't give you my reasons."

"Nevertheless," said Vendisson. "I now insist that this hospital be searched minutely. When such an accusation is made, I must see to it that it's cleared up beyond any shadow of doubt."

He swung to Kirkpatrick. "I demand that you bring up a detail of your men from headquarters—enough men to go through this building with a fine-tooth comb. And I want you to do it now, by telephone. Don't leave. I'll remain with you all the time, so no one may say that I slipped away to try to cover anything up!"

Kirkpatrick looked at Wentworth as if to say, "Well, see what your mad ideas have gotten us!" He said apologetically to Vendisson. "Please don't let this thing upset you. I have a good deal of affection for Dick, here, and I want to get him off the wrong track. I've never seen him so upset before."

Wentworth let him talk without bothering to reply. There was no use. All the possible harm had already been done. Nita's fate was now beyond changing.

The three of them went into Vendisson's office on the first floor. Vendisson motioned to the male nurse to follow them.

"And please do not speak to anyone as we go up, Rogan," he ordered. "I want nothing to happen that may cause Mr. Wentworth to suspect that I am trying to warn anyone in the building."

Up in his office, the doctor insisted that Kirkpatrick phone headquarters for a squad of men. Then the three of them waited, silently, in the office, with the male nurse standing in the window, his back to the room.

Wentworth's pulse was racing. His instinct had been right, in the first place, in not wishing to reveal his suspicions to Kirkpatrick. For he was a keen student of human nature, and he knew how the Commissioner would react. But his hand had been forced by Kirkpatrick. And now he couldn't tell what was happening to Nita.

In spite of the turmoil which surged up within him, Richard Wentworth forced himself to remain cool and observant. For one thing, he had listened to every single inflection of Vendisson's voice, comparing it mentally with the voice of Professor Secundus, which was etched in his memory.

WENTWORTH HAD trained himself to detect the subtle differences of voice, to catch the fleeting similarities of inflection and of tone in men's speech. But now he could detect no mannerism common to both Secundus and Vendisson. Either he was mistaken in his suspicion, either Nita was wrong, or else Vendisson was a superb master of voice control—which would not be so unusual in a surgeon of his attainments. Wentworth himself knew of a dozen ways of altering a voice, and he had done it countless times. For instance, the voice of the Spider was so distinctive—and so different from Wentworth's own normal voice—that men recognized it and feared it wherever it was heard.

But even while he was speculating on this idea, he was watching Rogan, the male nurse, at the window. When they entered, Vendisson had offered cigarettes from a humidor on his desk, which both Wentworth and Kirkpatrick had refused. The doctor had lit one, and then, as an afterthought, had offered one to the male nurse, who had accepted it gratefully. Now, the man was standing at the window and smoking. His right hand was visible to those in the room, but his left was in front of him.

Wentworth saw that there were almost imperceptible movements of the man's left shoulder, as if he were moving that left hand.

Wentworth moved around the room, and came up behind the nurse, making no sound upon the thick rug.

Vendisson, who had not spoken since Kirkpatrick made the telephone call, suddenly said, "Rogan! What time is it?"

Rogan jerked around, startled at the sharp tone, and almost jumped when he saw Wentworth so close behind him. He looked hastily at his wrist watch and said, "Twelve-forty, Doctor."

"Thank you, Rogan." Vendisson smiled apologetically at Wentworth and Kirkpatrick. There was a yellow-gold wristwatch upon his left wrist. He glanced down at it and said, "My watch has stopped working. Very inconvenient. Rogan keeps the time for me."

Wentworth said nothing.

In a few minutes, a squad of men arrived from headquarters, under Inspector MacGowan. When Kirkpatrick gave them instructions to go through every room, closet, ward and storeroom in the hospital, they looked their surprise.

"It's Wentworth's idea," Kirkpatrick explained fretfully. "He thinks Miss van Sloan and Miss Stanton are prisoners somewhere in the building."

MacGowan took it as a matter of routine. He issued orders to his men, and they dispersed, working in pairs.

When the room was emptied of police once more, Wentworth noted that Rogan had moved back, quietly, to the window.

Dick's eyes were grim. "Rogan," he said. "Will you oblige me by stepping away from that window?"

Rogan turned angrily. "Look here, Mr. Wentworth, I refuse to be treated like a criminal. If I want to stay here at the window, why you can't stop me—"

Wentworth took three quick steps which brought him face to face with the male nurse. He kept his eyes on the man, but reached his hand sideways, gripped the cord of the Venetian blind, and pulled it until the blind came all the way down to the sill.

Rogan said, "By God, I'll show you—"

And he swung with his right.

Wentworth smiled tightly. He moved his head a fraction of an inch, and the blow missed. He brought up his own right in a short arc that connected with the side of the man's jaw. Rogan's head snapped back with the sharp crack of the blow, and his eyes turned upward. His knees buckled, and he fell forward to the floor.

VENDISSON HAD leaped around from behind the desk, but he stopped short when Wentworth swung on him.

"Well, Doctor," Wentworth said softly. "Did you want to take a try at looking out of the window?"

Vendisson turned and looked helplessly at Kirkpatrick.

"I appeal to you, Commissioner. This man is going too far.

I don't mind allowing you to search the hospital. But when he presumes to dictate to my help, and strikes them—"

Kirkpatrick's eyes were glinting angrily at Wentworth. He started to speak, but caught himself up short as the office door opened and a young woman came in. She was breathtakingly beautiful, with black hair and black eyes, and a voluptuous figure which even the starched-white nurse's uniform could not hide.

She stopped abruptly just inside the door, and her eyes widened just a trifle at sight of Wentworth. Then she immediately covered them with her long, black lashes.

"I—excuse me. I didn't know I was intruding—"

"Come in, my dear," Vendisson said dryly, almost reluctantly. "Gentlemen, this is my daughter. Commissioner Kirkpatrick and Mr. Richard Wentworth."

"How do you do," she said in a stilted, brittle voice. "I just arrived at the hospital, and changed into nursing costume to assist you, father. And then I saw the police swarming around the place, so I hurried here to find out what was the matter."

Wentworth's blood was hot in his veins. Vendisson might have been an expert at disguising his voice. But his daughter was not so good. He would never forget that voice of hers, as long as he lived.

"I believe," he said slowly, "that we have met before."

She gave him a queer look. "I wouldn't be surprised."

She glanced at the prone figure of Rogan on the floor, flashed a hasty glance at her father, and said quickly, "Well, if you will excuse me, I must hurry—"

"Don't go," said Wentworth.

She stopped, with her hand on the door.

He stepped over and took her hand from the knob. "Just wait a few minutes longer," he said smiling. "Until they've finished searching the building. Then you may leave."

She gasped. "This is outrageous! Step out of my way!"

"Sorry," he said.

Kirkpatrick burst out angrily, "Look here, Dick, you can't do that. Doctor Vendisson has been good enough to permit us to search the hospital without a warrant. But we have no legal right to detain anyone here against their will. I'm sure Miss Vendisson is absolutely harmless. Let her pass."

"No," said Wentworth.

"By God then," Kirkpatrick exclaimed, "I'll put a stop to this whole silly business—" He stopped short at the sharp jangling sound of the telephone on Vendisson's desk.

The doctor picked up the instrument and said, "Yes?"

A sound filtered into the room which chilled every one there. It was sound of *laughter* coming through the receiver.

Vendisson jumped as if he had been stung. But at once, the laughter ceased, and a voice spoke. Everyone in the room recognized that voice, for they had heard it before, in radio broadcasts from a secret station which no one had ever been able to locate. The voice said:

"Vendisson, this is the Spider. Tune in at once on Station WKL!"

There was a *click,* and the phone went dead.

Vendisson put down the instrument, looking dazed. The

dark-haired Lona Vendisson turned and looked at Wentworth, and a sudden terror came into her eyes.

Wentworth pointed to the small radio behind Vendisson's desk. "Go on," he said, "Why don't you tune it in?"

VENDISSON WAS staring at him as if he were a ghost. Automatically, he backed around and twisted the dial. He caught Station WKL just on the tone signal, and then the announcer's voice came through the speaker, with a tight, strained note in it: "The broadcast regularly scheduled for this time will not be heard. Instead, you will hear an announcement by a gentleman who is here at my side now. I—I assure you that the station has had no hand in this. He—he is holding a gun to my head—"

The voice of the announcer was choked off, and another voice took its place. It was the sharp, strident voice of the Spider!

"Attention, New York!" he said. "This is the Spider broadcasting. Don't bother to send police here. I'll be gone before you can get started. I have a short message for the people of this city. You have been terrorized by Professor Secundus, who has abducted and blinded many of your loved ones. So fearful are you of this dreadful threat of blindness, that you are about to permit Professor Secundus to virtually take over the city. I say, do not permit it! I will tell you how to destroy this threat to yourselves and your dear ones. I will tell you the real identity of Professor Secundus. He is a man who has posed among you as a doer of good, as a dispenser of healing and medicine. But he has used his reputation to cloak the most vicious goal which ever an ambitious man entertained at the expense of the lives and happiness of a city. When I tell you this man's name, I call on you all to rise up and destroy him. Go to his place, and you will find the evidence of what I tell you. Then, take the law into your own hands. Do it tonight, before it is too late. For in the morning, one of your respected number is scheduled to ratify the doings of Professor Secundus over this very station. Richard Wentworth, who you all know and respect, finds himself in the power of Secundus because of danger to one he loves. Because his sweetheart is in danger of being blinded for life, or killed, he is going to address you tomorrow over this station, advising all to yield to Secundus, and not to thwart him. But I, the Spider, tell you that Wentworth is only human, and is doing this to save the life of one he loves more dearly than himself. Do not blame him. You can all understand why he will make the broadcast. I, too, understand!"

The sharp metallic voice of the Spider was silent for an instant, then went on with a new, a deep and understanding note.

"I, too have loved deeply, and have been ready to give up everything that made life worth while in order to save the one I loved. Believe me, people of New York, there is only one salvation for you from the merciless ambition of Professor Secundus. Go and destroy him! And now, I will tell you his name. He is the honored, the respected, the *devilish*—Doctor Adrian Vendisson! Now you know him. Now you know what to do. Hurry, lest he escape. For he has an autogiro on the roof of his hospital. Do not let him escape! That is all. This is the Spider, signing off!"

There was probably no one in that room who was more astounded than Commissioner Stanley Kirkpatrick.

For a long time now. Kirkpatrick had been privately convinced that his friend, Richard Wentworth, was the Spider. He had on many occasions tried to trap him, because it was his duty as Police Commissioner to apprehend the Spider. It was for this reason that he had been reluctant to go along with him on any blind venture tonight, and it was also for this reason that he had refused to return the serum to Wentworth. And he suspected that Wentworth was trying to pull the wool over his eyes by directing his suspicion toward Doctor Vendisson while he went after the real Secundus.

CHAPTER 11
COMING OF THE MOB

TO ONE thing Kirkpatrick could have sworn: that while Dick Wentworth was here in this room with him, the Spider was not anywhere else.

Therefore, it was a terrific shock to him to hear that the Spider was at this very moment at Station WKL. The Spider's voice was unmistakable. And the announcer himself had declared that the Spider was holding a gun on him.

What Kirkpatrick didn't know was that *both* voices—the announcer's and the Spider's—were the voice of the same man. Wentworth had spoken that whole speech into a record up in his apartment, before going down to meet Kirkpatrick. He had first enacted the frightened broadcast announcer, disguising his voice by using special mouth-plates.

Then, after changing the mouth-plates, he had reverted to the voice of the Spider, going on with his announcement.

It was this tricky record, with the two voices, which gave those in the room the illusion that the Spider had held up the announcer and was making a personal broadcast. Ram Singh had gone to WKL after dropping Wentworth and Kirkpatrick at the hospital. It was he who had held up the announcer, tying him securely. Then he had used the phone to call Vendisson, had played off another portion of the record in the Spider's voice, ordering him to tune in on WKL. Then the Sikh had merely moved the phonograph from the telephone over to the microphone, and let it play.

WKL was a small station, broadcasting mostly recorded programs, and did not have a large studio with the usual glass-enclosed engineers' booths. The microphone was in a small private office, and the technical apparatus in another room, so there had been no one present to observe Ram Singh's actions.

As the radio lapsed into silence, there was a hush as of death itself within that hospital room. Vendisson stood transfixed at his desk, staring with mingled disbelief and consternation at Wentworth. Lona Vendisson had a hand at her breast, and her eyes stared at Wentworth.

Both the Doctor and his daughter were positive that Wentworth was the Spider. They had themselves unmasked the Spider only this evening, and had seen beneath the make-up the features of this man who now stood in the room with them. Yet here was tangible proof that the Spider was another man. Doubt began to fill the eyes of Vendisson. He had thought that Wentworth was only bluffing, earlier in the evening, when he had denied being the Spider, and when he had denied having been in the Riverdale house. Now he was beginning to wonder....

BUT THE thing that must have struck Doctor Adrian Vendisson with even greater force, was the nature of the things which the Spider had told the people of the city in his broadcast. Even though the Spider was himself a wanted man, there were thousands of men and women in New York who had faith in him. And in the present mood of the people, they would only be too eager to believe one like the Spider. It would not be long before the first rumblings of the mob came to be at the doors of the Vendisson Eye and Ear Hospital. Many of them might not be fully convinced, but they would come to convince themselves.

It was Kirkpatrick who spoke first. He said, "Dick! I—I—you—that was the Spider!"

"Yes," Wentworth said, "and he bears out what I told you about Vendisson, here. Perhaps you will listen to the Spider."

Kirkpatrick came closer to him. "But Dick, it *couldn't* be the Spider." He looked squarely at him. *"Because I know where the Spider is at this moment!"*

Wentworth shrugged. "You're too obstinate, Kirk. If you won't believe the evidence of your ears, I can't argue with you. The point is, that Vendisson here, is Professor Secundus. And his charming daughter is no less guilty than he."

"Preposterous," said Vendisson. "Wentworth is in league with the Spider. For some reason, they are conspiring to ruin my reputation. I demand that you do something about this, Commissioner!"

There was a rap at the door, and Inspector MacGowan entered.

MacGowan said, "My men have covered every nook and cranny of this hospital. We can't find a trace of Miss van Sloan or Miss Stanton. Everything seems to be in order."

"All right," barked Kirkpatrick. "Take your men outside and form a cordon around the hospital. Phone headquarters for reserves. There may be a mob here at any minute. The Spider is causing trouble. He just broadcast a statement that Vendisson is Professor Secundus!"

"Whew!" exclaimed MacGowan. "We're in for it now!" He hurried across to the phone and dialed headquarters.

Vendisson stepped forward, with a glow of righteous indignation in his eyes.

"Commissioner," he exclaimed, "I demand the arrest of Richard Wentworth on the ground that he assaulted my man here, who is still unconscious from the blow, and on the further ground that he has attempted to create a disturbance in a hospital, endangering the lives of my patients!"

Kirkpatrick shrugged. "You have a right to have him arrested, Doctor. As for my part, I agree with you. If you wish to make a formal complaint, I'll have him placed in custody."

"I do!" said Vendisson.

"Very well." Kirkpatrick motioned to a detective who was standing in the hall. "Arrest Mr. Wentworth, Scott. Take him downtown and book him on a charge of simple assault, and of creating a disturbance in a hospital."

"Wait, Kirk!" Wentworth said. "Don't do anything you'll regret. Whether I'm right or wrong about Vendisson, don't forget that Nita and Mary are still in the hands of Professor Secundus. I've got to be free to help them."

"I'm sorry, Dick," Kirkpatrick said gruffly. "You're all wrought up. In your present condition you're liable to do them more harm than good."

Detective Scott came up

NITA VAN SLOAN

145

and put a hand on Wentworth's shoulder. "I'm sorry, Mr. Wentworth, you're under arrest."

LONA VENDISSON was looking at him with strange, intense eyes. There was a little smile of triumph twisting at her full and sensuous lips, and looking at her, Wentworth could read the message of her eyes: *Well, you fool, while you're safely in a cell, I'll be attending to your precious Nita!*

She came up close to him and said, "Do you know what I'm thinking, Mr. Wentworth?"

"I'm sure I do!" he said.

She shrugged, and stepped past him. "Perhaps we had better go and attend to the patients, father," she said. "They will be needing attention—with all this excitement."

"Yes," Vendisson said, with a slow smile. "They will certainly be needing attention. Let us go and take care of them!"

"Go ahead," said Commissioner Kirkpatrick. "Go right ahead, Doctor. But I advise you not to leave the building without a police escort. There may be trouble with the mob."

"I shall not be leaving for a little while, Commissioner," Vendisson said with a little side-glance at Wentworth. "There is—ah—some business I must attend to first."

He stepped out of the office, following his daughter.

MacGowan put down the phone and said to Kirkpatrick, "The reserves are on the way, sir. I'll go out and dispose the men I have with me. I've ordered tear gas, in case any real trouble should develop."

The Commissioner nodded. "You and Scott take Wentworth down with you. Send him to headquarters in a police car."

"Look here, Kirk," Wentworth said desperately. "I've never asked you for a favor before. I'm asking one now. Don't place me under arrest. I have to be free now. Vendisson and his daughter are going to kill Nita and Mary."

Kirkpatrick sighed. "I'm afraid the strain has affected you, Dick. You yourself heard MacGowan report that everything was in order here. The girls are not in the building. And Vendisson is remaining here. Even if your wild accusations were true, and Vendisson *were* Professor Secundus, how could he do anything to Mary and Nita, when they're not even in the hospital?"

"I don't know yet, Kirk," Wentworth said passionately, "but I swear to you that I'm right. Somehow, Vendisson is going to kill Nita, because she knows he's Secundus!"

He saw the pained look in the face of his friend, and he also saw the knowing glance exchanged between Detective Scott and Inspector MacGowan. They thought that worry and excitement were causing him to have delusions.

"Better come along, Mr. Wentworth," Scott said in kindly fashion. "A good night's sleep will do you a world of good."

"And you can depend on us, Dick," Kirkpatrick added, "to do everything in our power to save Nita."

Wentworth kept his burning, passionate protests pent up within himself. He saw that it was no use trying to convince these men that Nita was somehow going to be killed under their very noses. He had failed to prove his startling charge that Vendisson was Professor Secundus, and they would listen to him no more. Even if subsequent events proved him right, it would still be too late, because Nita would be dead. If the

Spider's words were to succeed in arousing a mob, the police would disperse it, and the people of the city would certainly think that Secundus had the authorities under his thumb. They would dumbly resign themselves to the terror of the Professor, realizing their helplessness.

BUT HE said none of this to Kirkpatrick. All he said was, "Don't you owe me a break, Kirk? These charges aren't serious. You know I'm responsible. Parole me in my own custody till the morning, and I'll agree to appear in court and answer the complaint."

"No, Dick. It's for your own good that I'm putting you in a cell tonight. It'll keep you out of trouble."

He motioned to Scott and MacGowan, and they ranged themselves on either side of Wentworth, each taking him by an arm.

Dick wondered if it would do any good to tell Kirkpatrick that if he were placed in a cell tonight, without a chance to find Professor Secundus' secret cache of serum, he'd be stone blind by morning. But he decided against it for two reasons. First, the Commissioner was in no mood to believe anything he told him. In the second place, the pride of Richard Wentworth would not permit him to make such an appeal. His lips tightened. He said nothing. Silently, he permitted Scott and MacGowan to lead him from the room.

The hall was filled with MacGowan's men, waiting for further orders. There was no sign of Doctor Vendisson or his dark-eyed daughter. Then MacGowan turned to Wentworth.

"I'm sorry as hell about this, sir—"

148

Wentworth wasn't listening. There was a grim, hard look in his eyes. If only they'd hurry, and take him away in a squad car, he might have a chance to overpower his guard and return. Even then, it might be too late. And they'd be a cordon around the hospital, making it difficult, if not impossible, to re-enter.

That feeling of utter helplessness which he had experienced once before, this evening, assailed him again, with even greater force. In a moment he would do something desperate, make one crazy try for freedom—if only for a few moments....

His tight, terrible thoughts were disturbed by an ominous sound which, rising in the near distance, was swiftly approaching and gaining in volume and crescendo.

Through the glass doors of the main hospital entrance he could see a great mass of humanity approaching, in broken, straggling array, heading in their direction. The sound of a thousand voices filled with bitter anger, floated toward them on the night air. That vague, darkly blurred mass of people in the night was coming to storm the hospital.

It was the mob—the mob which he himself had evoked by his recorded broadcast.

The Spider's voice had aroused the city!

CHAPTER 12
SATAN'S PRIVATE HELL!

"GOOD GOD!" exclaimed MacGowan. "They got here fast!" He raised his voice. "Snap it up, boys! Get out there and stop that mob! Turn on all the squad car spotlights.

Flood them with light. But don't hurt anyone if you can help it. I'll be right out there and talk to them!"

He swung to Wentworth. "We can't take you out now. We'll have to hold you here... Scott, take him to one of the private rooms and keep him there!"

He was already on the run as he shouted that last order, and he disappeared outside to endeavor to control the *mob*. Their angry voices were already filtering through into the hospital, and the frightened staff were scurrying around through the lobby in the grip of panic.

Scott looked at Wentworth and shrugged. "I guess I have to stay in here with you, Mr. Wentworth. Come along."

He led him to the rear of the foyer, then along a side corridor, looking for a room where they might wait. This side corridor opened into a vaulted passage which apparently led out of the building, and Wentworth wondered where it would take one. Then he remembered that the Empire Crematory adjoined the hospital, and that it was connected with it.

At the very same instant that this thought occurred to him, another idea hit him with the full force of frightful realization. He blanched at the implication of the idea he had just gotten, and he stopped stock still, staring down that dark and vaulted corridor.

Nothing was too grotesque to believe about Professor Secundus. And this idea which he had just gotten was indeed grotesque—and terrible.

Scott looked at him queerly. "What's the matter, Mr. Wentworth?"

"Look here, Scott," Dick exclaimed. "I think I've figured out just how Vendisson is going to dispose of the bodies of Nita and Mary. *He's going to cremate them!*"

The detective stared at him with wide and incredulous eyes. "My God, Mr. Wentworth! You've really gone mad!"

"No, no!" exclaimed Wentworth. "I wish to Heaven I *were* mad. I wish it weren't real. That crematory next door—that's the answer. I've been stymied because you didn't find anything in the hospital. But I didn't know the layout here. I just remembered that the crematory is next door to the hospital. It's their land that this place is on. And it's in there that Vendisson conceals his prisoners. It's in there that he's busy destroying the evidence against him—destroying human beings who could incriminate him—under your very noses! Let's go!"

"Nothing doing!" Scott shouted. "You're crazy! Here—come in this room—"

Scott seized him by the arm, and dragged him toward a room just off the corridor.

Wentworth's lips tightened. His body became taut, steel-spring muscles reacting with a speed spurred on by this desperation. He brought his fist up in a hard jolt to Scott's jaw. The detective was jerked backward by the blow, and Wentworth stepped in, struck him once behind the ear. Scott dropped like a log.

WENTWORTH CAST a swift glance up and down the corridor. No one was in sight. The hospital staff was congregated out in front, in the lobby, watching the police battle to keep the angry mob in check. Hoarse and maddened shouts were tear-ing from the throats of those in the mob as they surged against the police line.

"*We want Vendisson!*" they shouted and screamed. "*We want Vendisson!*"

The reserves had already arrived, and tear gas bombs were ready. Kirkpatrick's voice could be heard trying to shout down to them from the upper floor window, trying to get them to listen. And a crew of police were setting up a machine-gun in the foyer in case the mob overcame the police outside. In the foyer, a dozen bells were ringing, as patients up above tried vainly to get some attention. Blind men and women up there, unable to see, unable to find their way around, were frightened at the sounds arising from that mob.

Already, Wentworth was far down at the end of the corridor, at a locked door barring further progress into the crematory next door. Wentworth worked at that door with desperate, frantic fingers. In his apartment, he had provided himself with all the implements he needed, as well as with a complete Spider outfit. His flat black case of Swedish steel implements was in his hand, and within a minute, the door became no longer an obstacle. It yawned open, upon a stairway leading down into a dark and foul-smelling basement.

Wentworth paused only long enough to slip on his cape and hat. He did not bother with makeup. But upon his face he fitted a plastic-rubber mask molded into the familiar features of the Spider. It was an emergency mask, which would pass in a pinch, but would never do at close quarters. Now it would have to serve. That feeling which Wentworth had experienced out in the lobby, was now stronger than ever. He could have staked his life that he would find Nita and Mary Stanton down there. Whether they would be still alive, he did not know.

The door closed behind the shadowy figure which descended the stairs soundlessly. Richard Wentworth had disappeared.

It was not Richard Wentworth who went down into the basement of that crematory, but the black and avenging figure of the Spider—grim and merciless fighter, with two automatics, black as the black-gloved hands which held them....

IT WAS very dark down here where Nita was lying, and the floor was cold and hard, and there was a chill which penetrated to the very marrow of her bones.

She could see nothing when she opened her eyes, and for a moment she thought that she was blind.

A great shudder went through her as she thought back over the evening. First, there was the car in which she had sat with Doctor Vendisson and that daughter of his, whose eyes always burned with a terrible hate when she looked at Nita. She remembered that she had accepted Vendisson's invitation to visit the hospital, hoping to get some clue to the fate of Dick Wentworth, by interrogating Jack Blair. But in Vendisson's office she had begun to feel the subtle change in the man, the enveloping aura of evil which emanated from him. Queer, that she hadn't noticed it before. The man knew how to act. In public, he was the reserved, dignified surgeon. Only in private, with a victim who would never be able to speak again, did he permit the bubbling lava of evil within his soul to boil to the surface.

Nita had seen that, then. But it was too late. There were two male nurses in the office, and at a signal from Vendisson they had seized and gagged her, and placed her on a stretcher and strapped her into it, and trundled her through the hall, down here. And Nita remembered the hot and burning, and triumphantly vindictive eyes of Lona Vendisson, fixed upon her implacably as she was taken from the office.

She knew then that she was to die, and she knew why.

It was later that Vendisson had come with the male nurses and ungagged her, but left her strapped. They had taken her into a little room with a phonograph recording device.

Vendisson had carefully explained to her that Dick Wentworth would be blind by morning if he did not receive another injection of serum. To prove what he said, he showed her the various objects which had been taken from the Spider that evening in the Riverdale house. She knew then that he was telling the truth.

"But you can save him, my dear. I am demanding a hundred thousand dollars ransom for you. Speak a message to him into this record. I'll play it for him over the phone. Tell him it is useless to resist, that he must pay. If you do that, and he takes your advice, my dear, I'll give him the antidote for blindness."

Looking into the hateful eyes of Doctor Vendisson, Nita knew that he was lying to her, that he would never let her leave this place alive, and that he would not keep his word with Dick. But she must dissemble, she must spar, she must be clever, for Dick's life and his eye sight hung in the balance. For herself she did not care. If only she could convey a warning to Wentworth!

"Let me think for a few minutes," she said.

Vendisson smiled. "Ten minutes, my dear. Here, we will unstrap your right arm. There is paper and pencil. Write the message in your own words, for Wentworth will know your style well enough to judge whether it was dictated to you, or you did it of your own free will. I want him to believe that the advice you give him is your sincere and considered opinion."

So Nita took the pencil and began to scribble, and her thoughts took shape, and she began to feel cold all over lest when Vendisson return, he discover the thing she was trying to do.

But he saw nothing suspicious in the message, though he studied it carefully. To make sure that it would be harmless, he changed several words here and there.

"All right. You may speak it into the phonograph."

The change of words did not disturb Nita. Her problem was to accentuate certain ones in such a way that Vendisson would not notice, but that Dick would. She closed her eyes as she spoke the piece, concentrating upon the Morse Code, which Dick had insisted upon her learning with the proficiency of a telegraph operator.

THE MALE nurses took her back to the dark cell and laid her on the floor, removing the straps. She shuddered, feeling their coarse hands upon her body.

One of them said, "Baby, you got what it takes!" He laid eager, stubby fingers on the white skin of her shoulder.

Nita's violet eyes flamed, her cheeks flushed. She twisted away, and struck him.

The man snarled, while his companion laughed, and came at

The Spider's automatics swung on the gunmen in white.

156

her with a hot, lustful fire in his eyes, and tongue licking at his lips. He backed her to the wall, then reached one hand to her shoulder and the other to the front of her dress to rip it away.

Nita had learned boxing and *jiu-jitsu* from Dick Wentworth. She raised both her hands, seized his right wrist, and twisted. The man's body came off balance. He uttered a hoarse cry as he tried to right himself. The cry was cut off in the middle as Nita raised her left hand and brought the edge of it down sharply upon a spot at the side of his throat, a little behind, and about an inch and a half below, the right ear. The man stiffened, and collapsed at her feet.

But Nita had been so preoccupied with defending herself against this one that she had no time for the other. That one stepped in, grinning, and a revolver appeared in his hand. He reversed it and brought the butt down on her head in a hard blow.

Nita's breath escaped from her lips in a gasp, and she sagged forward, slipping down along the wall to the floor where she lay in a crumpled heap.

The man who had hit her bent and helped his companion to his feet, led him, wobbling, out of the cell. He turned out the light inside, and locked the door.

"You'll be all right in a few minutes, Toby," he said. "That dame hit you a nice one. It was cute. Boy, is she a spitfire!"

"Yeah!" snarled Toby. "I'm going back in there when she wakes up. I'll break her, all right!"

But Nita was to be spared at least this indignity. For when she finally opened her eyes to the utter blackness about her—a blackness so deep that for a moment she thought they had blinded her—events were taking place near by, of which she was unaware. Though she did not know it, Dick Wentworth was in the hospital next door, pleading with Kirkpatrick for a chance to look for her. And police were crowding in the corridors of the hospital.

The light in her cell suddenly went on, blinding her for an instant with its powerful incandescent glare. Then she saw Toby and the other male nurse opening her door. Behind Toby was the sinister, gaunt-faced Doctor Vendisson, perspiring a little now, and urging the male nurses to hurry. And looking into the cell over Vendisson's shoulder was the black-haired, vindictive Lona. She was watching Nita with a deep, sadistic appreciation, and her red lips were curved into a witch's smile.

The two nurses seized Nita, and dragged her out of the cell. She didn't struggle with them. Wentworth in many lectures, had taught her not to waste energy in futile exertions against impossible odds. Nita saw that it was useless to offer resistance now. In addition to these two male nurses, there were others in the hall outside the cell. She could easily be overpowered, and in the struggle she might even be rendered unconscious, so that when the crucial moment came she would be powerless to help herself. SHE LET them take her into the corridor, and then she uttered a cry, for she saw little Mary Stanton, also in the grip of white-coated male nurses.

"Hurry," Doctor Vendisson said to his men. "There is very little time. The police are all over the hospital, and they may even be clever enough to think of searching this crematorium."

He smiled unpleasantly, and motioned to the men, who seized both Nita and Mary, and forced them down upon their backs, each on a pine board, six feet long and two feet wide, which were on the floor. Nita heard Mary Stanton cry out, and then she heard a blow, and Mary was silent. She could not see what they had done to the mayor's daughter, for she was being strapped to the pine board, with the straps running across her chest and her legs. And in a flash she knew what was going to be done to her! A single word had given her the clue. She had not known where she was. Now she did. Vendisson had said—*crematorium!*

Horror filled Nita's eyes as the pine board upon which she lay was lifted by two men, carrying it like a stretcher. They moved down the corridor, with Doctor Vendisson leading the way.

Lona Vendisson walked alongside Nita's stretcher. She looked down at the bound, beautiful girl, and her black eyes glittered with a strange and terrible light.

"Wentworth is in the hospital next door," she said to Nita, with a sharp edge to her voice. "But it isn't going to help you. Maybe someday I'll show him your ashes—after he's forgotten you, and gone away with me!"

Nita looked up at her, pityingly. "You—love Dick Wentworth?" she asked.

"Yes!" Lona spat. "He's the only man in the world I've ever wanted. When you're gone, I'll make him love me. I know how to do it—as long as you're not in his mind!"

Nita smiled sadly. "How could you go to him, with murder on your hands?"

Lona laughed. "My father brought me up like this. He taught

me to hate—but never to love. Now I can do both. I love Richard Wentworth—and I hate you!"

Nita closed her eyes. She was surprised to be able to think dispassionately. It was ironical that she was to come at last to her death because of the man who loved her. Were it not for the strange and terrible passion which Wentworth had somehow, unconsciously, aroused in the breast of this savage girl who had been raised by her father without a vestige of moral restraint, Nita would not be condemned to death now.

She opened her eyes and found that Lona was watching her like a hawk.

"Afraid?" Lona asked her eagerly. "Frightened? Terrified of dying?"

Nita smiled. "Afraid? No. I don't want to die, Lona, but I'm not afraid of death. I'll cheat you of that much, at least. You won't see me cringe."

Lona's lips shut tightly, and she looked away.

THEY WERE swinging into a small, vaulted room, and Nita twisted her head around to see where they were. At one end of the room there was a huge Siemens regenerative furnace, one of the latest types used in crematories. She could see the massive pipes leading into the cremating chamber, pipes which sent a hot blast of heated hydrocarbon to mix with the air and raise the temperature of the chamber to 2000 degrees Centigrade. The walls of the chamber were white-hot, all ready to receive the first body for cremation.

The male nurses carried her, still strapped to the pine board, up on the small platform directly in front of the oven aperture.

They placed her on the platform and stepped back. This platform was equipped with a lever which, when pushed over, tipped the platform, sending the body sliding into the furnace. The hot blast which emanated from the oven aperture was almost unbearable here, the super-heated metal casting a deep red glow upon Nita's face and body, and reflecting from all the walls of the room. Nita began to feel her skin scorching from the heat, even now, outside the furnace.

She looked up and saw Vendisson standing close to her, next to his daughter.

Vendisson was smiling.

"You are going to be first, my dear. Mary Stanton will follow you." He waved to a shelf upon which rested a row of black metal urns. "I will see to it that Wentworth receives your ashes, my dear—after I have made myself master of the country. It is too bad that he would not join me. I could have used him. As it is, he will soon have no choice but to take orders from me—or to become blind for the rest of his life. I am sure that my daughter will soon be able to make him forget you."

Nita forced a smile. She knew that Dick would never forget her. She knew that Dick would surely avenge her—if he survived. But the thought of his being blind was even more terrible to her than the thought of her own imminent death. Even now she was thinking, plotting for some idea, something she could do now that would help Dick after her death.

"Perhaps you've made a mistake," she said. "Something you overlooked, Doctor, in your long and careful plans."

He frowned. "What is that?"

"The serum. You no doubt have it stored in the hospital. The police will find it."

He shook his head. Amusement showed in his gaunt face.

"No, my dear. The police will not find it. It's stored right here, in the crematorium. You see, bodies are embalmed here. In the next room, there are two barrels marked Embalming Fluid. Those barrels contain my serum. The police will never be clever enough to analyze that embalming fluid. Kirkpatrick believes me to be the most public-spirited citizen in the city. So much so does he believe it, that he has just placed your friend, Wentworth, under arrest for creating a disturbance in the hospital, by charging that I am Professor Secundus. I confess, I don't know what made him suspect me. I shall have to question him about that—when he comes to beg me for serum!"

A GREAT surge of satisfaction filled Nita's heart, in spite of the hungry furnace waiting for her body. Then Dick had caught the hidden meaning in her message. Her effort had not failed! At least she had done her modest share in the good fight. And she had an overwhelming confidence that Dick Wentworth would find a way to win the battle against this gaunt man who called himself the reincarnation of Satan, and his evil daughter.

"And now, my dear," Doctor Vendisson said, "the time has come!"

He stepped up on the ledge alongside the platform, towering over her, and reached for the lever which would tilt the platform toward the glowing, white-hot furnace chamber. In the reflection of that glow from the furnace, he looked like some necromancer of the Middle Ages, come to earth to work his evil magic with modern machinery. His hand reached the lever.

"Wait!" Nita gasped. "You—aren't you going to—kill me, first?"

Vendisson laughed, but did not answer. The reply came from alongside the platform, where Lona Vendisson was standing, with the white-coated men behind her, watching the scene with avid, sadistic eyes.

"No," said Lona Vendisson. "We're not going to kill you first. We're going to watch you shrivel in that heat—alive. Now—don't you want to beg for a quick death?"

Nita swallowed hard. "No!" she said. "Go ahead and push that lever!"

A flicker of disappointment darkened the eyes of Lona Vendisson—disappointment, and perhaps bitter rage that she could not break down this proud and beautiful girl whom Wentworth loved. Perhaps in that instant, when she saw the spirit and the pride of Nita van Sloan in all its glorious beauty, she understood that she, herself, could never command the love of the man who loved Nita. Balked out of the spiteful satisfaction of seeing Nita cringe, she was seized with a dreadful rage that sent surges of fiery color up her throat.

"Damn you!" she shrieked, and leaped up on the ledge alongside her father. "Push that lever!" She slipped around in front of Vendisson, and snatched at the lever.

"Throw her in—"

Suddenly, she froze, with the screaming words dying in her

throat. Her eyes were fixed in utterly incredulous fascination upon the doorway at the other side of the room.

Doctor Vendisson jerked around to look in that direction, as did the other white-coated men in the room.

A gasp seemed to rise from all their throats in unison.

Only Nita van Sloan smiled a tight, strained little smile.

For that terrible cloaked figure which stood in the doorway was an ominous specter of death-dealing doom to all but Nita. The black cape swirled about the figure of the Spider, and out from under the turned-down hat-brim gleamed a pair of eyes that were terrible in the intensity of their glittering impact. From under the black cape poked the noses of two dull-burnished automatics.

"The Spider!" someone gasped.

Vendisson's long and flexible surgeon's fingers dived under his coat and came out with a small pistol. His gaunt face was twisted into a mask of satanic fury, while behind him, his daughter's features became contorted by rage into a ghastly travesty of her dark and sensuous beauty. The white-coated men in the room dived for their guns, too.

THE SPIDER did not move from the doorway. But those implacably glittering eyes of his were everywhere, saw everything; saw, for instance, that Vendisson had but to pull the lever toward him in order to slant the platform and send Nita sliding into the white-hot furnace.

So the first shot from the Spider's automatics smashed into the body of Vendisson, into his stomach, so that the impact would carry him forward *against* the lever, instead of pulling it toward him.

And then the Spider's guns swung on the gunmen in the white coats, thundering their rhythmic threnody of death in repeated blasts that sent wave after wave of deep-throated roaring sound to shatter against the walls, while the snub-nosed bullets thudded with deadly accuracy into the bodies of those cornered rats.

Their own guns belched, but they were held in shaking hands. These men had seen that terrible light in the eyes of the Spider, under his hat-brim, and they knew that they were facing death. They pulled their triggers quickly, desperately, frantically, without taking the time to aim. And the Spider stood there in the doorway, a weird and ominous figure, disdaining to take cover, disdaining to crouch, only standing and shooting those thundering guns like a cold and efficient fighting machine.

He did not look toward the platform, for his eyes were seeking out enemies through the powder-smoke.

But up on that platform, a terrible thing was happening.

The Spider's shot had sent Vendisson hurtling into the lever, and he clawed at his daughter for balance. She, eager to seize that lever, pushed him a little, and he lost his footing on the ledge alongside the platform. He went toppling forward, directly toward the aperture of the white-hot oven.

A scream of pure, unadulterated terror gurgled in the throat of this man who called himself the reincarnation of Satan, and he clutched wildly at Lona's dress. His frantic fingers snatched, and found, a hold upon her sash. He clung frantically, and his weight dragged her backward, throwing her, also, off balance. She screamed, and for a moment they both hung teetering over the edge of the platform, directly above Nita's bound body.

Desperately they clawed at each other and at the air, twisting, shrieking, emitting ghastly, discordant sounds of terror. Then they both went over, straight into the white-hot furnace. Their cries, which had been drowned by the thundering gunfire, were now blotted out entirely. The white heat in the interior of the oven increased in intensity for a moment, then subsided. A frightful stench filled the room.

Nita closed her eyes, and pressed the lids down hard, trying to blot from her mind's eye the terrible thing she had just witnessed. And suddenly, the shooting ceased....

She opened her eyes, and looked.

The Spider was still in the doorway. No other man was standing in that room. And on the floor, none of the bodies moved or twitched. The Spider had shot to kill, tonight.

The eyes of Nita van Sloan met those of the Spider across the room. They said nothing to each other, because Mary Stanton was watching them, lying strapped to her pine board, at the foot of the platform. And the things they had to say to each other now were not for the ears of Mary Stanton, or of anybody else in the whole wide world.

Mary had gone through the entire ordeal as through a nightmare, terrified and speechless. She had seen Vendisson and his daughter hurled into the crematory furnace by the Spider's bullet, she had crouched against the leather straps which bound her while gunfire had thundered in the room. And now, with her wide eyes fixed upon the black-caped man in the doorway, she began to shiver.

SLOWLY, THE Spider returned the two heavy, empty automatics into unseen holsters beneath the cape. Then he crossed the room and bent over Nita, removing the straps which were cutting into her breasts and her thighs and her knees.

"Dick!" she whispered. "I—saw them fall into the furnace. I—shall never get rid of the picture!"

He nodded grimly. "I never thought I'd get to you in time, darling. I'm going now. Kirkpatrick and the others will be here as soon as they break in the door from the hospital. I jammed the lock. And there's work to do. I must locate the serum—"

She smiled. "It's in here, Dick, in one of the storerooms. Two barrels of it, labeled *Embalming Fluid.*"

He pressed her arm. "Good girl. Take care of Mary Stanton. I'll be back."

He helped her off the platform, then hurried out of the room, stopping only to bow to Mary Stanton who cried, "Spider! You saved our lives!"

Then he was gone from the room. Out in the corridor, he stripped off mask and hat and cape. At the end of the corridor, an acetylene torch was being applied to the door he had jammed.

Wentworth smiled. He slipped into a dark corner just as the jammed door was burst in, and police trooped into the place, with Kirkpatrick at the head. From outside, the angry cries of the mob could be heard, battling with the police. Kirkpatrick and his men rushed past Wentworth's corner without ever seeing him. Wentworth slipped in at the tail end of the line, alongside of Detective Scott.

Scott swung around, saw him, and uttered an exclamation. "Mr. Wentworth! You'll get me in trouble. I don't mind you're hitting me. You had a right to try to escape. But if the Commissioner knows you got away from me, he'll demote me—"

Wentworth smiled. "Need he ever know?"

Scott brightened.

Wentworth went on softly, "You see, I'm still your prisoner!"

"Thanks!" said Scott. He took Wentworth's arm and they followed the crowd of uniformed men into the furnace room.

Kirkpatrick was looking a little dazed, listening to the stories of Nita van Sloan and Mary Stanton.

He saw Wentworth and hurried over to him! "Dick! I owe you an apology!"

Wentworth gazed at the room with a good imitation of surprise, elation and wonder. "Nita!" he exclaimed, and went over and took her in his arms. "I'd given up hope for you!"

He turned and took the hand of Mary Stanton, who was close to them. "And you, too, Mary. What happened here?"

The mayor's daughter shuddered. "Vendisson and his daughter were cremated in their own furnace. The—the Spider saved us. He came in and shot it out with these men!"

"I see," said Wentworth.

KIRKPATRICK, HIS face flushed with excitement, turned and spoke to Detective Scott. "Never mind Wentworth any more, Scott. He's discharged from custody. Go out there to that crowd. Tell them they have nothing more to fear from the blindness—thanks to the Spider. Tell them there's enough serum in here to cure any of their dear ones who have been blinded. Hurry, or they'll break through the lines and tear the building down!"

When Scott was gone, Kirkpatrick took Wentworth aside. "You know. Dick, I owe you an apology on more than one point. I was sure—I could have staked my life on the moral certainty—that *you* were the Spider. Especially when we got a phone call from Station WKL saying that the whole Spider broadcast was recorded, and that the Spider himself had never been there."

He paused and smiled. "But now—there's the story of Mary Stanton. She says it was the Spider who shot it out with these men, and saved her and Nita."

"Well?" Wentworth asked, smiling.

"Well, it *couldn't* have been you, Dick," Kirkpatrick grinned. "Because you were in the custody of one of my own men all the time. So shake on it, Dick, and let's go find that serum. We can get some city physicians to administer it to all the patients up in the hospital."

Wentworth winked at Nita as he followed the Commissioner. "I think," he said, "that I'll take a dose of that serum myself—just for the experience!"

And Nita van Sloan winked back at him.